Dance Class

Béka • Writer

Crip • Artist

Maëla Cosson • Colorist

Miami

Dance Class

Studio Danse [Dance Class]
by Béka and Crip
©2023 BAMBOO ÉDITION.
www.bamboo.fr
English translation and all
other editorial material
© 2023 Published by
Mad Cave Studios and Papercutz.
www.papercutz.com

DANCE CLASS #13
"Swan Lake"
BÉKA — Writer
CRIP — Artist
MAËLA COSSON — Colorist
MARK McNABB — Production
JOE JOHNSON — Translation
WILSON RAMOS JR. — Lettering
STEPHANIE BROOKS — Editor
REX OGLE — Editorial Director
JIM SALICRUP
Papercutz Editor-in-Chief

Special thanks to
CATHERINE LOISELET

Papercutz was founded by
Terry Nantier and Jim Salicrup.

ISBN: 978-1-5458-1127-6

Printed in China
September 2023

First Papercutz Printing

Laura Chacón – Founder, Mark London – CEO and Chief Creative Officer, Mark Irwin – Senior Vice President,
Mike Marts – EVP and Editor-in-Chief, Chris Fernandez – Publisher, Rex Ogle – Editorial Director of Papercutz, Zohra Ashpari – Senior Editor,
Stephanie Brooks – Editor, Giovanna T. Orozco – Production Manager, Miguel A. Zapata – Design Director, Diana Bermúdez – Graphic Designer,
David Reyes – Graphic Designer, Sebastian Ramirez – Graphic Designer, Adriana T. Orozco – Interactive Media Designer,
Nicolás Zea Arias – Audiovisual Production, Cecilia Medina – Chief Financial Officer, Starlin Gonzalez – Accounting Director,
Kurt Nelson – Director of Sales, Allison Pond – Marketing Director, Maya Lopez – Marketing Manager, James Faccinto – Publicist,
Geoffrey Lapid – Sales & Marketing Specialist, Spenser Nellis – Marketing Coordinator, Chris La Torre – Retail Relations Manager,
Christina Harrington – Direct Market Sales Coordinator, Pedro Herrera – Retail Associate, Frank Silva – Executive Assistant,
Stephanie Hidalgo – Office Manager

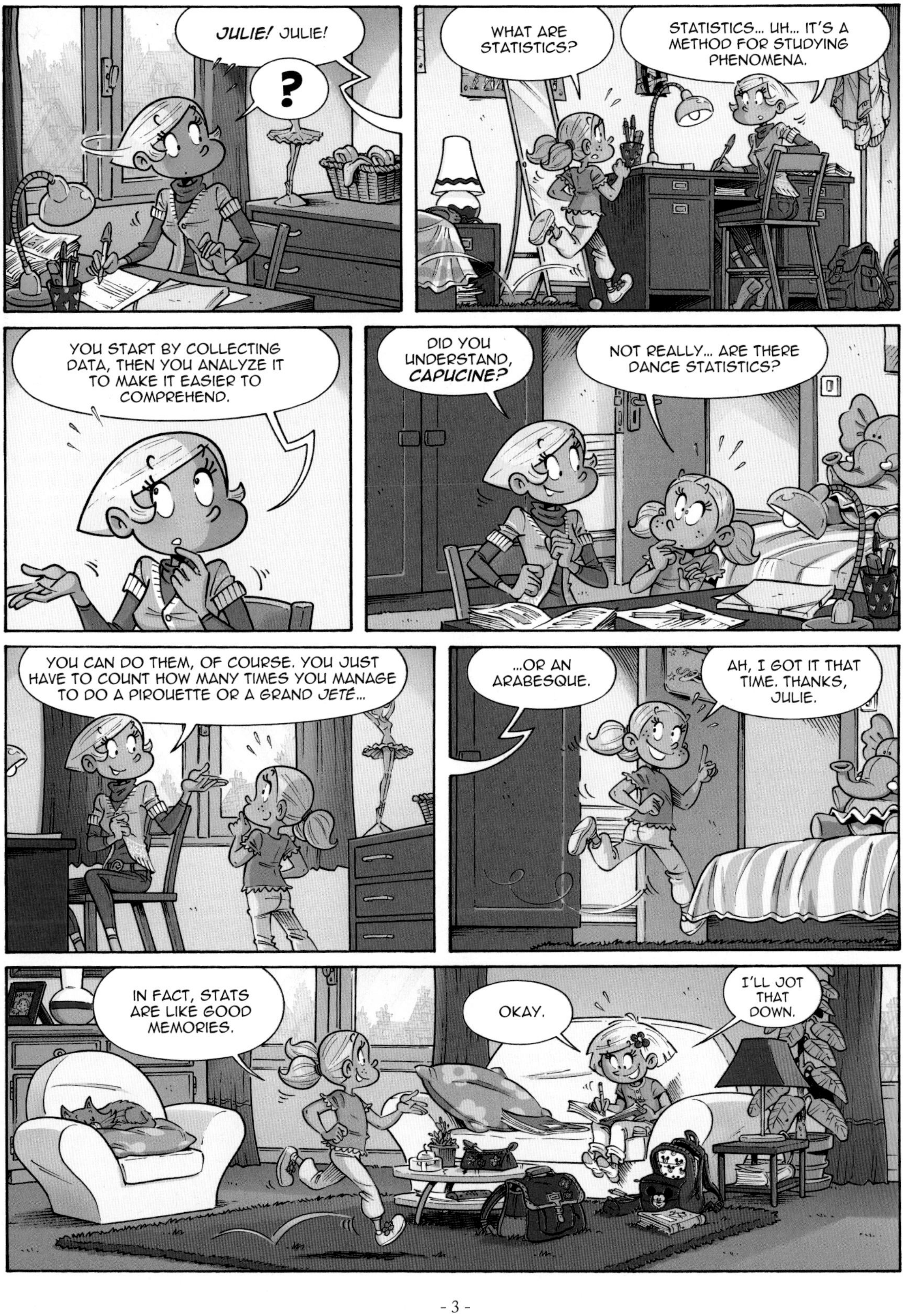
JULIE! JULIE!
?
WHAT ARE STATISTICS?
STATISTICS... UH... IT'S A METHOD FOR STUDYING PHENOMENA.
YOU START BY COLLECTING DATA, THEN YOU ANALYZE IT TO MAKE IT EASIER TO COMPREHEND.
DID YOU UNDERSTAND, CAPUCINE?
NOT REALLY... ARE THERE DANCE STATISTICS?
YOU CAN DO THEM, OF COURSE. YOU JUST HAVE TO COUNT HOW MANY TIMES YOU MANAGE TO DO A PIROUETTE OR A GRAND JETÉ...
...OR AN ARABESQUE.
AH, I GOT IT THAT TIME. THANKS, JULIE.
IN FACT, STATS ARE LIKE GOOD MEMORIES.
OKAY.
I'LL JOT THAT DOWN.

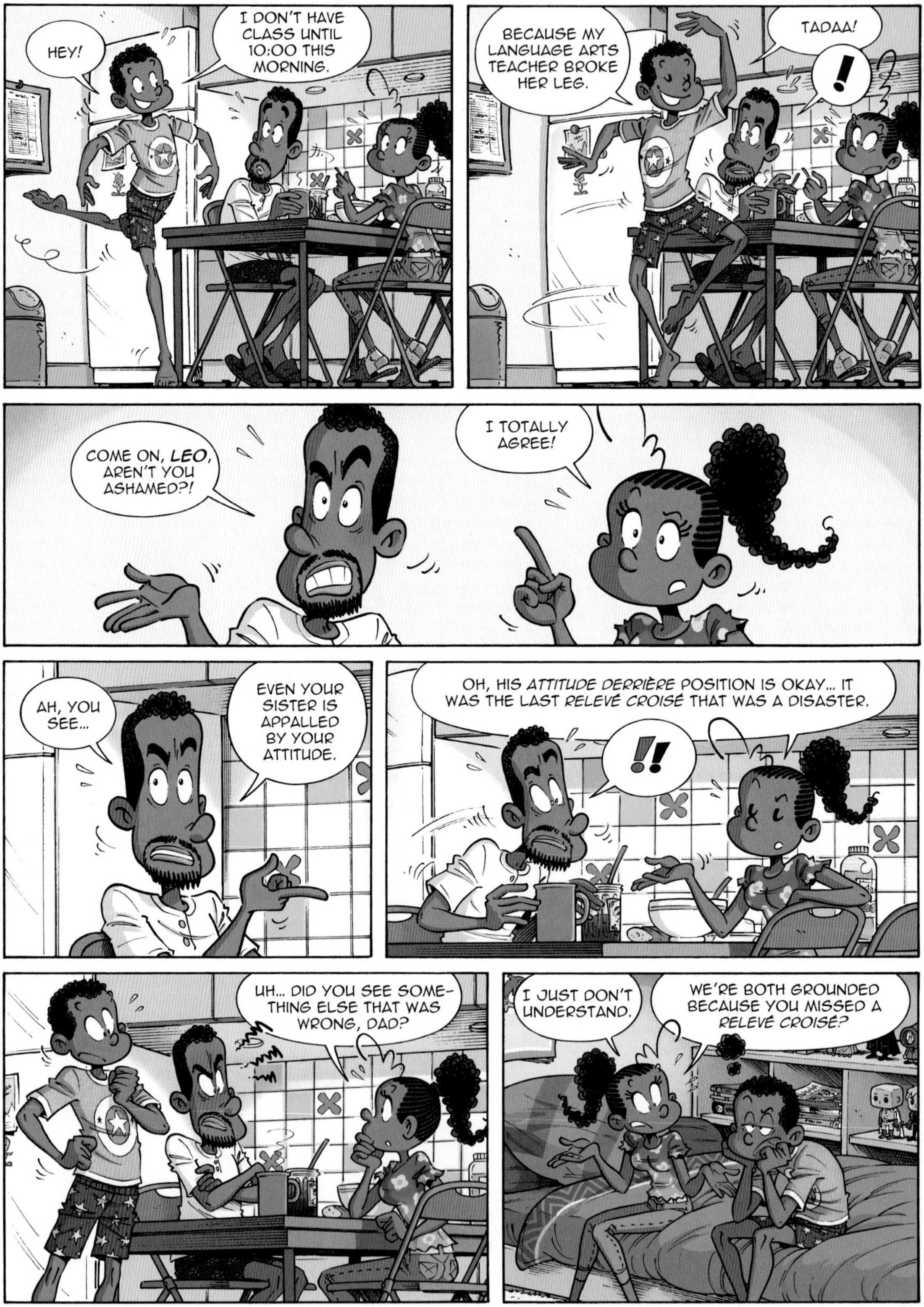
HEY!
I DON'T HAVE CLASS UNTIL 10:00 THIS MORNING.
BECAUSE MY LANGUAGE ARTS TEACHER BROKE HER LEG.
TADAA!
!
COME ON, LEO, AREN'T YOU ASHAMED?!
I TOTALLY AGREE!
AH, YOU SEE...
EVEN YOUR SISTER IS APPALLED BY YOUR ATTITUDE.
OH, HIS ATTITUDE DERRIÈRE POSITION IS OKAY... IT WAS THE LAST RELEVÉ CROISÉ THAT WAS A DISASTER.
!!
UH... DID YOU SEE SOMETHING ELSE THAT WAS WRONG, DAD?
I JUST DON'T UNDERSTAND.
WE'RE BOTH GROUNDED BECAUSE YOU MISSED A RELEVÉ CROISÉ?

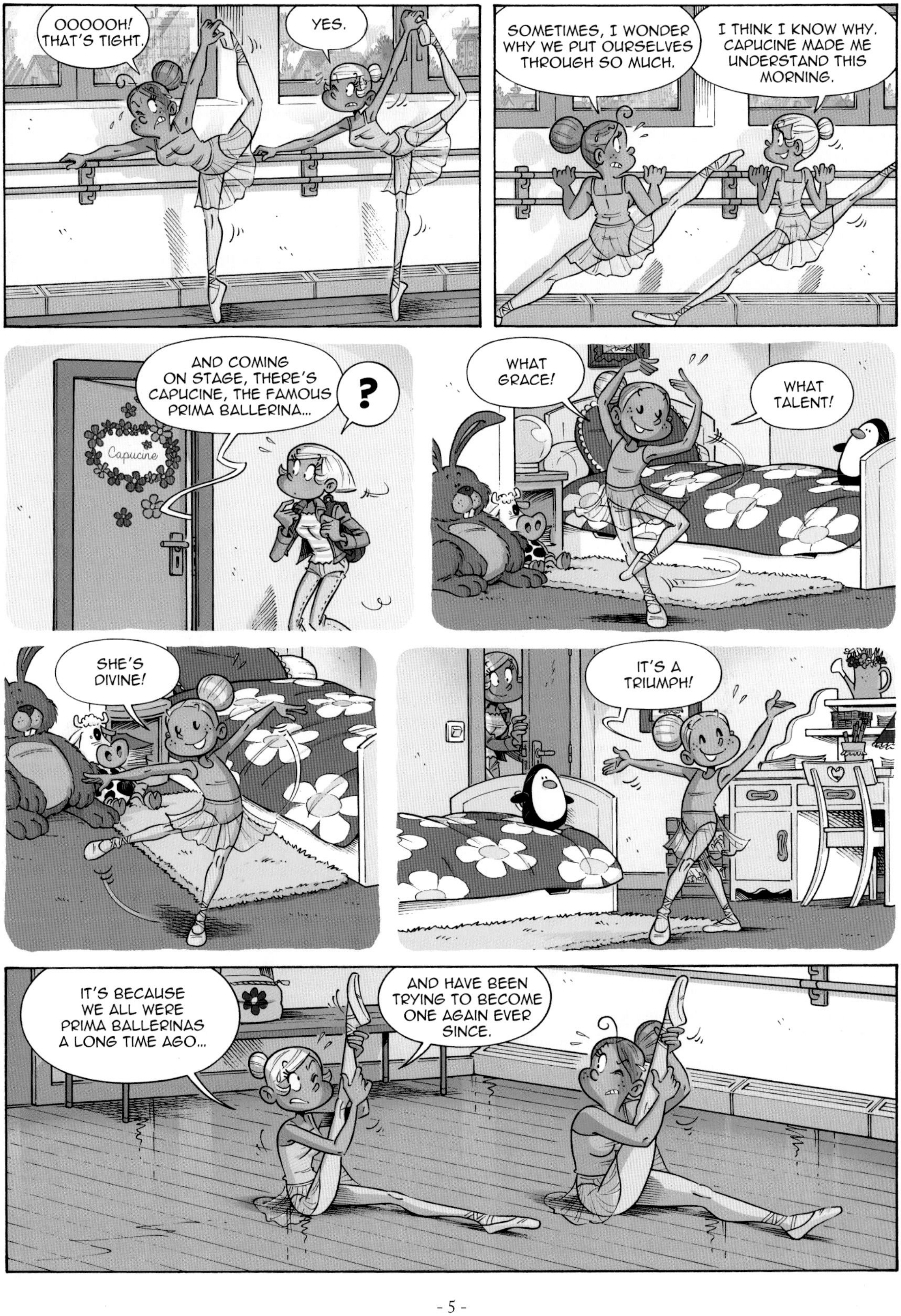
OOOOOH! THAT'S TIGHT.
YES.
SOMETIMES, I WONDER WHY WE PUT OURSELVES THROUGH SO MUCH.
I THINK I KNOW WHY. CAPUCINE MADE ME UNDERSTAND THIS MORNING.
Capucine
AND COMING ON STAGE, THERE'S CAPUCINE, THE FAMOUS PRIMA BALLERINA...
?
WHAT GRACE!
WHAT TALENT!
SHE'S DIVINE!
IT'S A TRIUMPH!
IT'S BECAUSE WE ALL WERE PRIMA BALLERINAS A LONG TIME AGO...
AND HAVE BEEN TRYING TO BECOME ONE AGAIN EVER SINCE.

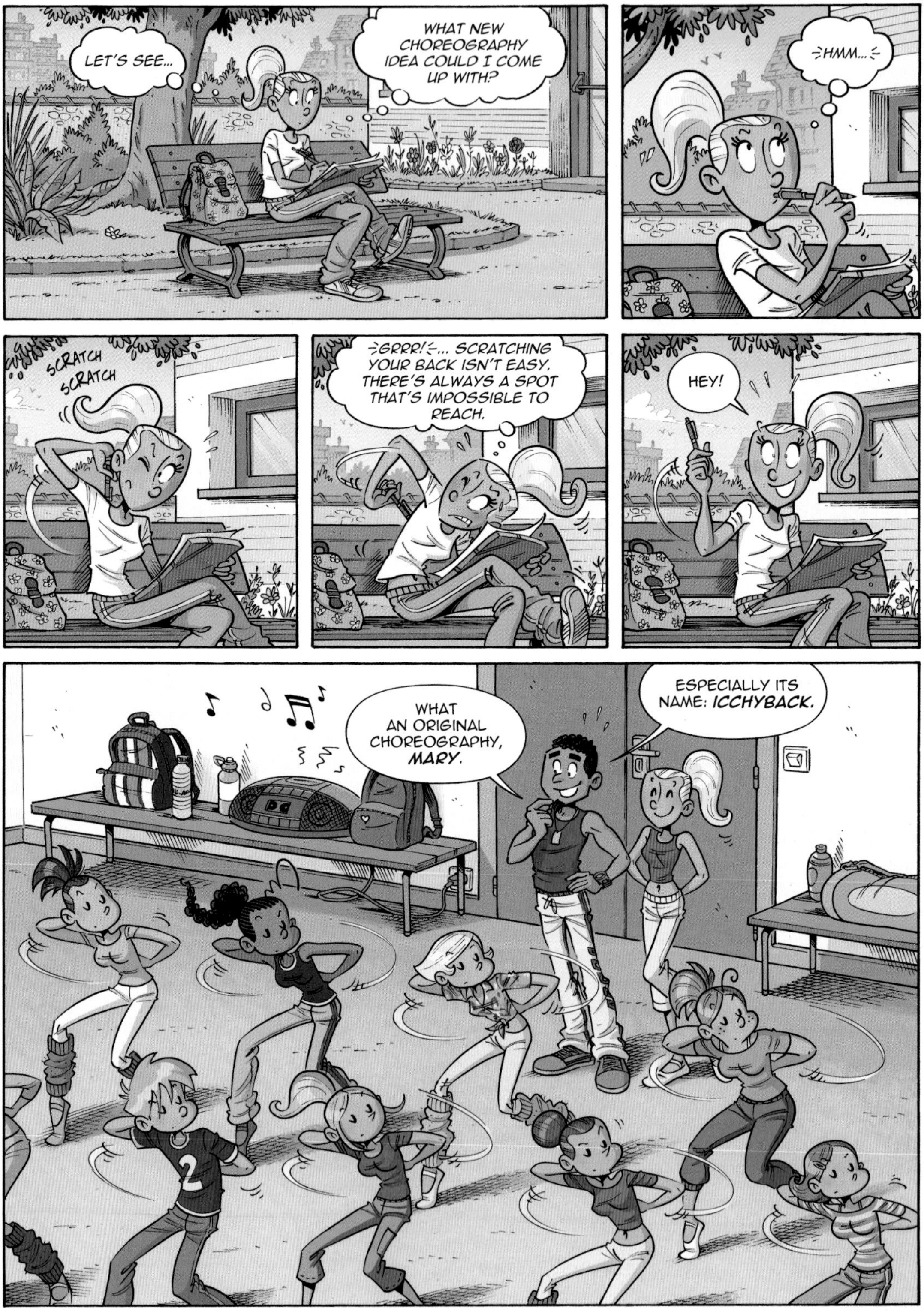
LET'S SEE...
WHAT NEW CHOREOGRAPHY IDEA COULD I COME UP WITH?
HMM...
SCRATCH SCRATCH
GRRR! ... SCRATCHING YOUR BACK ISN'T EASY. THERE'S ALWAYS A SPOT THAT'S IMPOSSIBLE TO REACH.
HEY!
WHAT AN ORIGINAL CHOREOGRAPHY, MARY.
ESPECIALLY ITS NAME: ICCHYBACK.

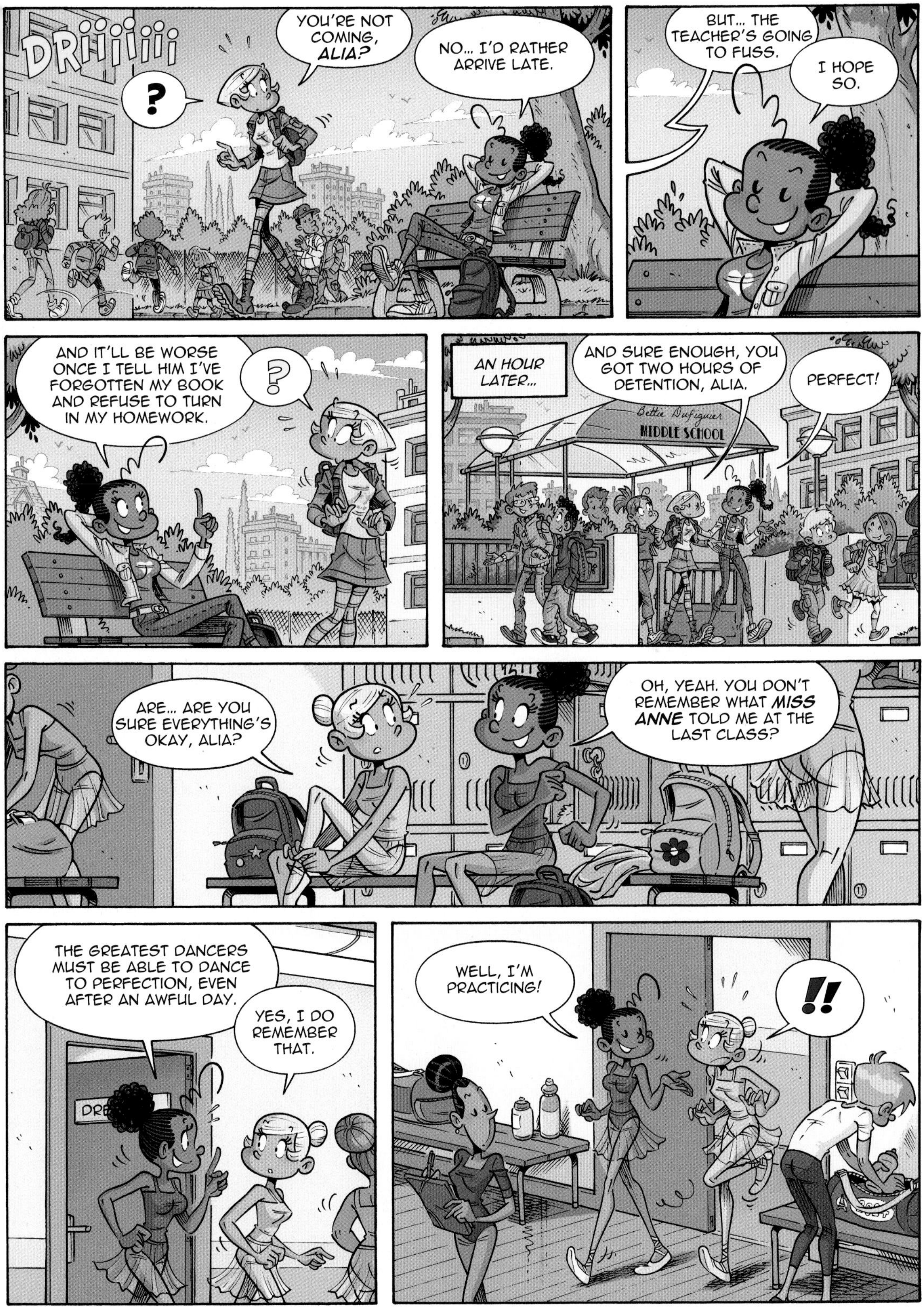
DRIIIIIII
?
YOU'RE NOT COMING, ALIA?
NO... I'D RATHER ARRIVE LATE.
BUT... THE TEACHER'S GOING TO FUSS.
I HOPE SO.
AND IT'LL BE WORSE ONCE I TELL HIM I'VE FORGOTTEN MY BOOK AND REFUSE TO TURN IN MY HOMEWORK.
?
AN HOUR LATER...
Bettie Dufiguier
MIDDLE SCHOOL
AND SURE ENOUGH, YOU GOT TWO HOURS OF DETENTION, ALIA.
PERFECT!
ARE... ARE YOU SURE EVERYTHING'S OKAY, ALIA?
OH, YEAH. YOU DON'T REMEMBER WHAT MISS ANNE TOLD ME AT THE LAST CLASS?
THE GREATEST DANCERS MUST BE ABLE TO DANCE TO PERFECTION, EVEN AFTER AN AWFUL DAY.
YES, I DO REMEMBER THAT.
WELL, I'M PRACTICING!
!!

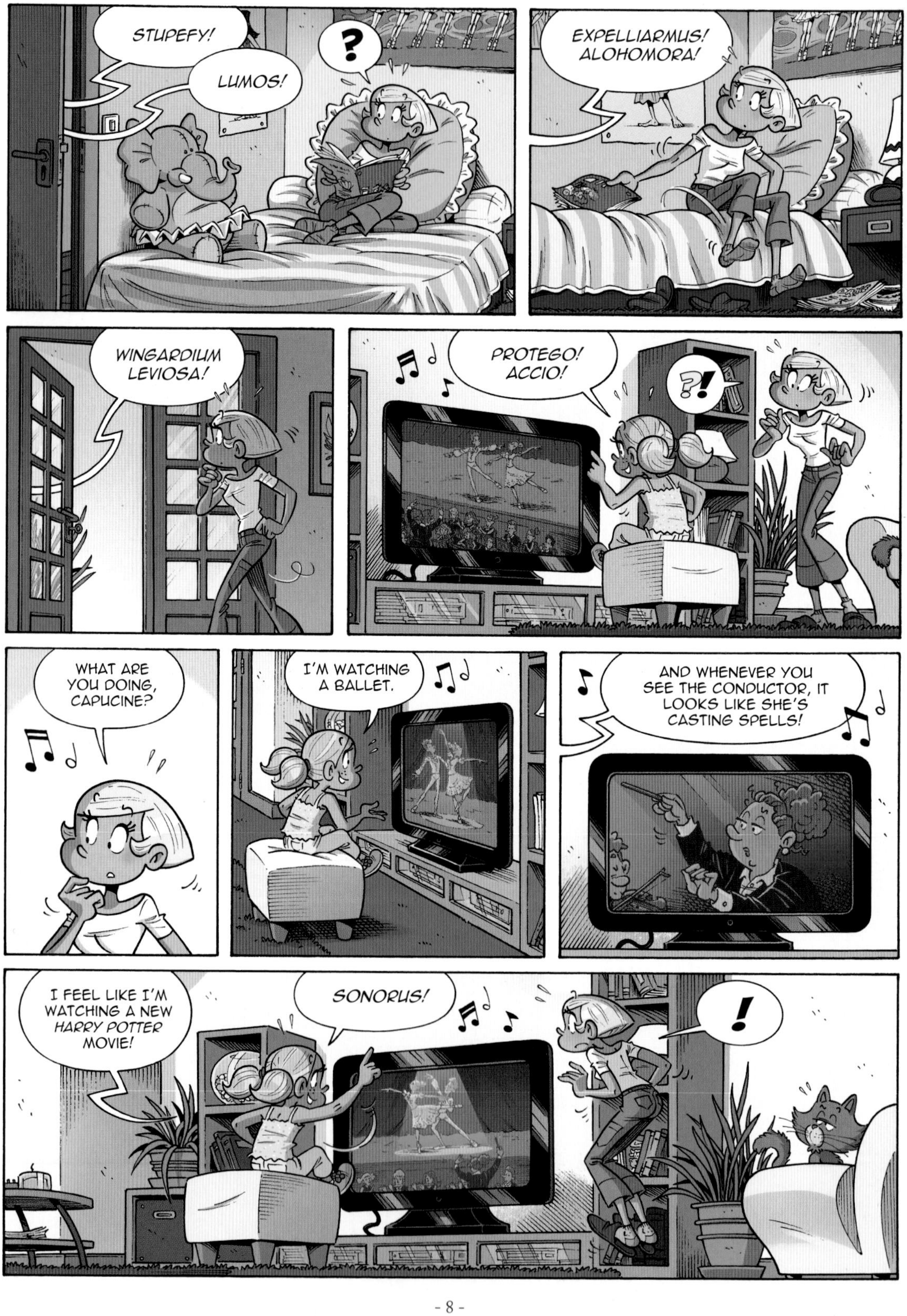
STUPEFY!
LUMOS!
?
EXPELLIARMUS! ALOHOMORA!
WINGARDIUM LEVIOSA!
PROTEGO! ACCIO!
?!
WHAT ARE YOU DOING, CAPUCINE?
I'M WATCHING A BALLET.
AND WHENEVER YOU SEE THE CONDUCTOR, IT LOOKS LIKE SHE'S CASTING SPELLS!
I FEEL LIKE I'M WATCHING A NEW HARRY POTTER MOVIE!
SONORUS!
!

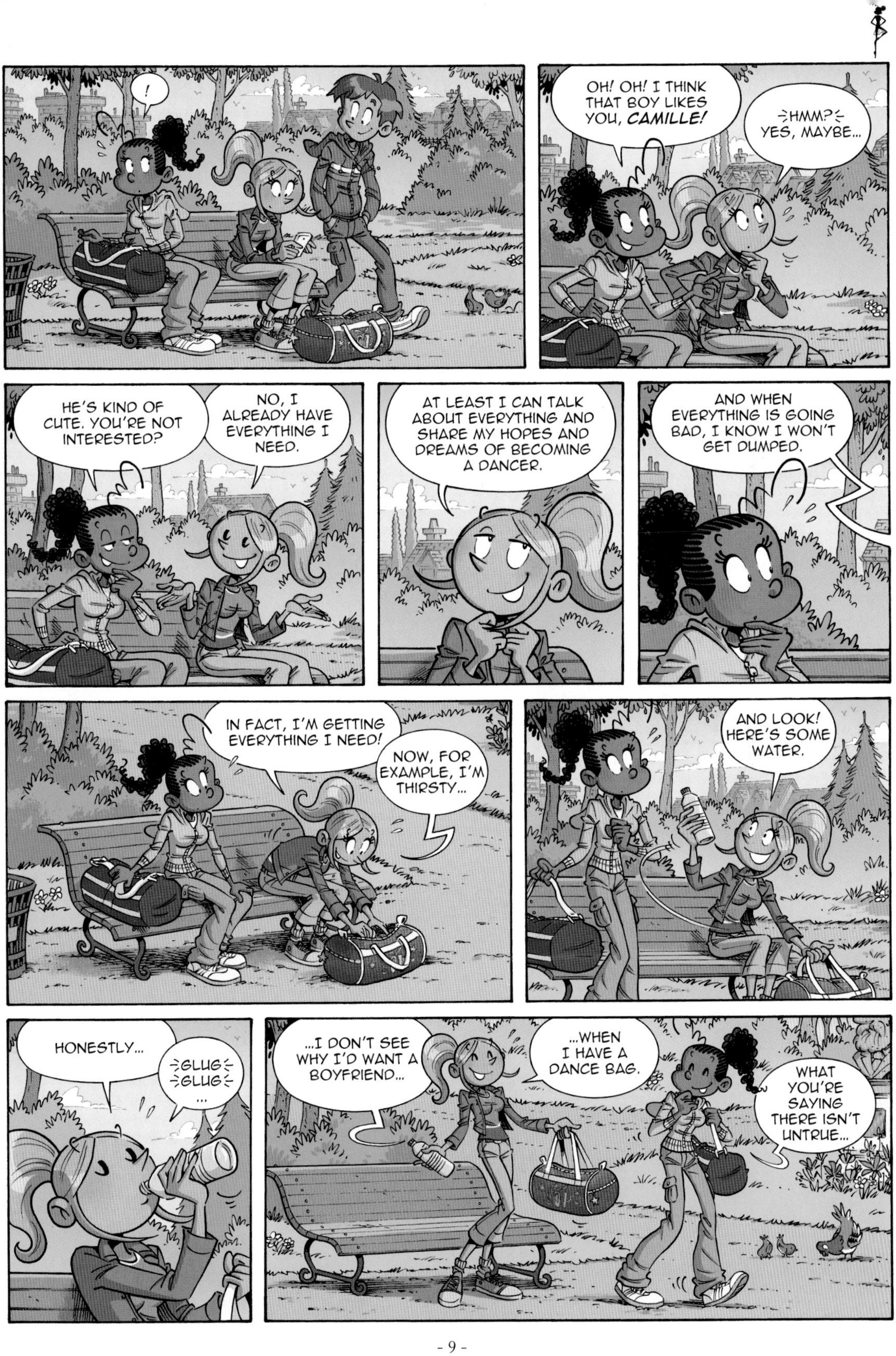
!
OH! OH! I THINK THAT BOY LIKES YOU, CAMILLE!
HMM? YES, MAYBE...
HE'S KIND OF CUTE. YOU'RE NOT INTERESTED?
NO, I ALREADY HAVE EVERYTHING I NEED.
AT LEAST I CAN TALK ABOUT EVERYTHING AND SHARE MY HOPES AND DREAMS OF BECOMING A DANCER.
AND WHEN EVERYTHING IS GOING BAD, I KNOW I WON'T GET DUMPED.
IN FACT, I'M GETTING EVERYTHING I NEED!
NOW, FOR EXAMPLE, I'M THIRSTY...
AND LOOK! HERE'S SOME WATER.
HONESTLY...
GLUG GLUG ...
...I DON'T SEE WHY I'D WANT A BOYFRIEND...
...WHEN I HAVE A DANCE BAG.
WHAT YOU'RE SAYING THERE ISN'T UNTRUE...

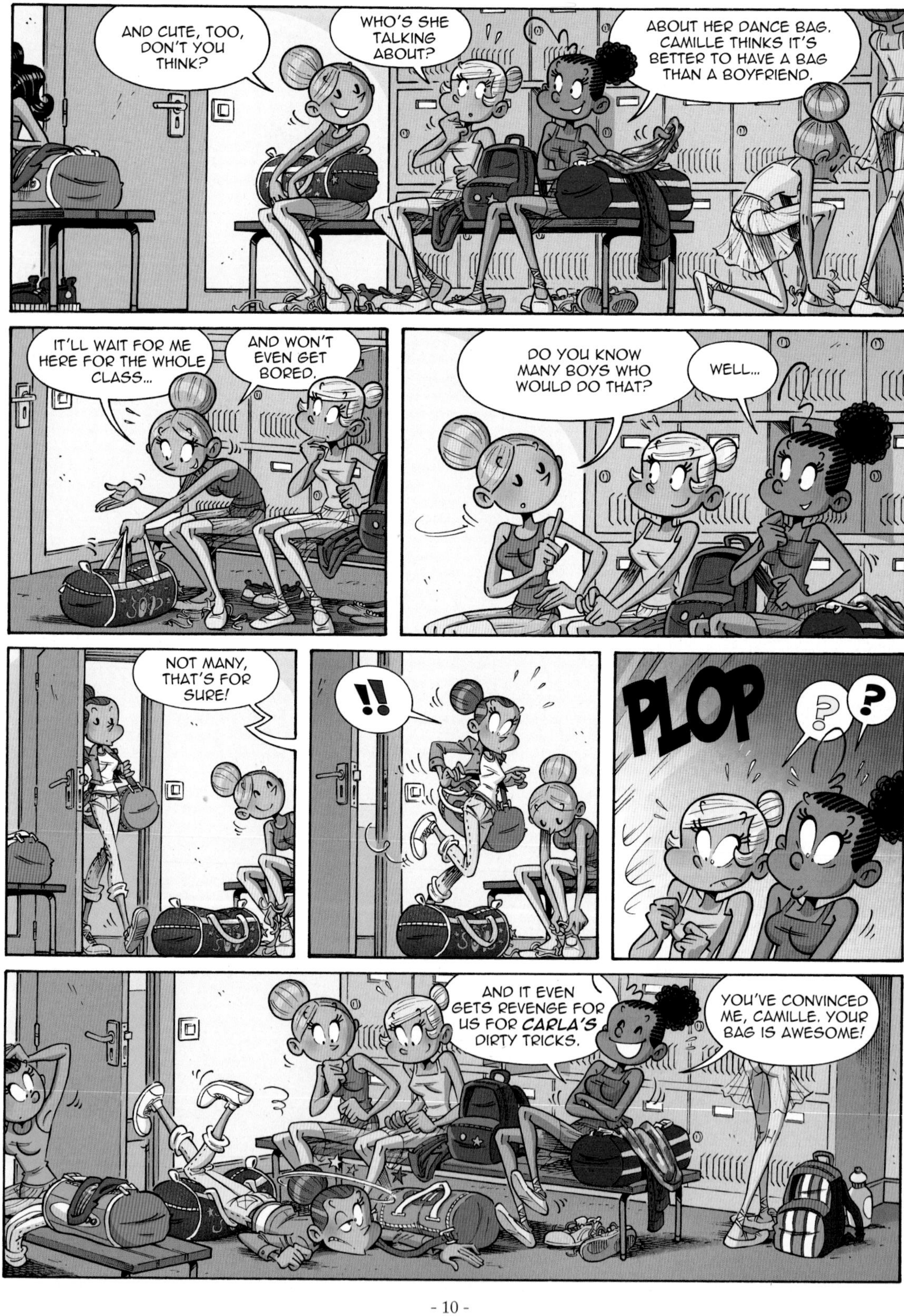
AND CUTE, TOO, DON'T YOU THINK?
WHO'S SHE TALKING ABOUT?
ABOUT HER DANCE BAG. CAMILLE THINKS IT'S BETTER TO HAVE A BAG THAN A BOYFRIEND.
IT'LL WAIT FOR ME HERE FOR THE WHOLE CLASS...
AND WON'T EVEN GET BORED.
DO YOU KNOW MANY BOYS WHO WOULD DO THAT?
WELL...
NOT MANY, THAT'S FOR SURE!
!!
PLOP
?
?
AND IT EVEN GETS REVENGE FOR US FOR CARLA'S DIRTY TRICKS.
YOU'VE CONVINCED ME, CAMILLE. YOUR BAG IS AWESOME!

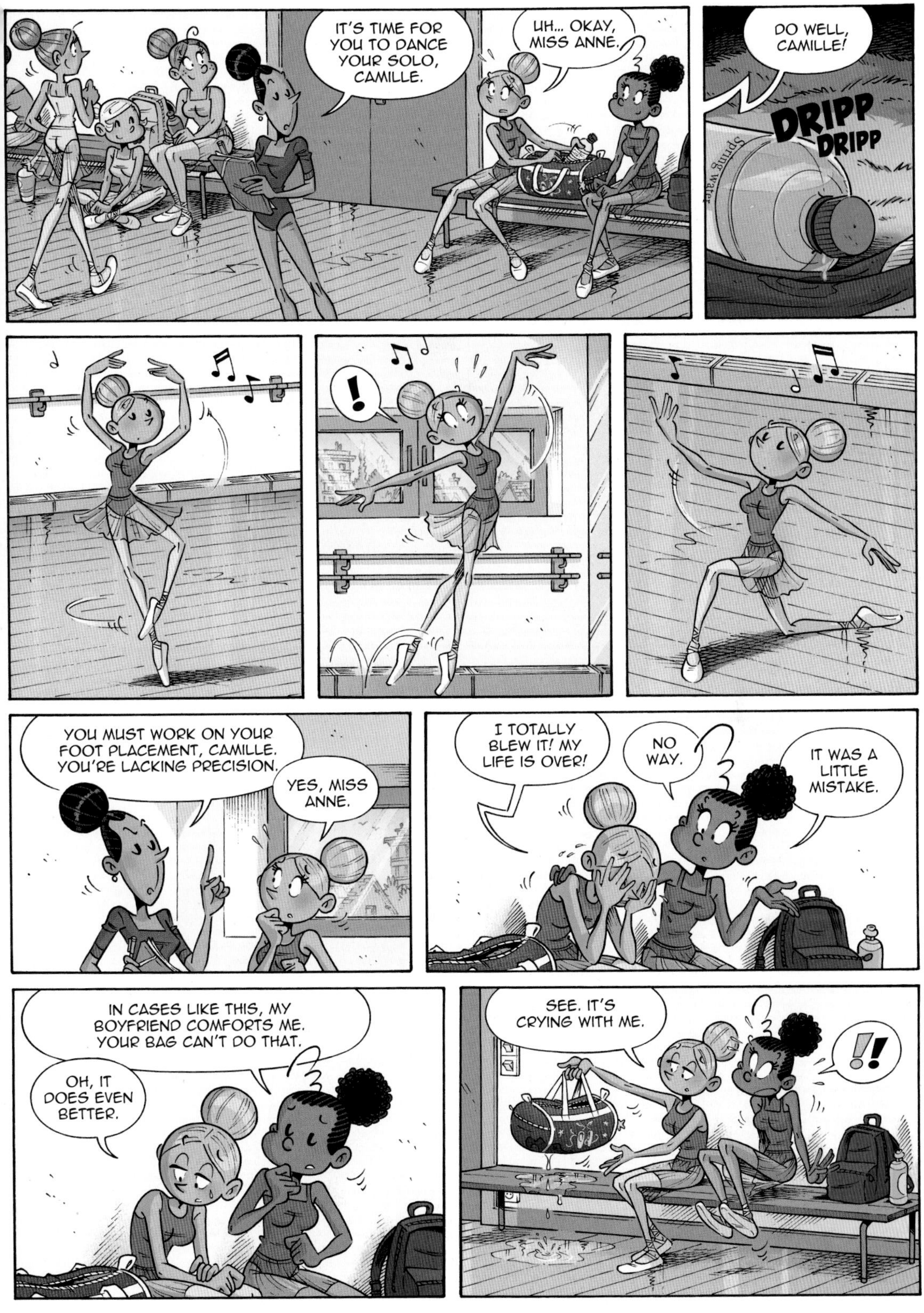
IT'S TIME FOR YOU TO DANCE YOUR SOLO, CAMILLE.
UH... OKAY, MISS ANNE.
DO WELL, CAMILLE!
DRIPP
DRIPP
Spring water
!
YOU MUST WORK ON YOUR FOOT PLACEMENT, CAMILLE. YOU'RE LACKING PRECISION.
YES, MISS ANNE.
I TOTALLY BLEW IT! MY LIFE IS OVER!
NO WAY.
IT WAS A LITTLE MISTAKE.
IN CASES LIKE THIS, MY BOYFRIEND COMFORTS ME. YOUR BAG CAN'T DO THAT.
OH, IT DOES EVEN BETTER.
SEE. IT'S CRYING WITH ME.
!!

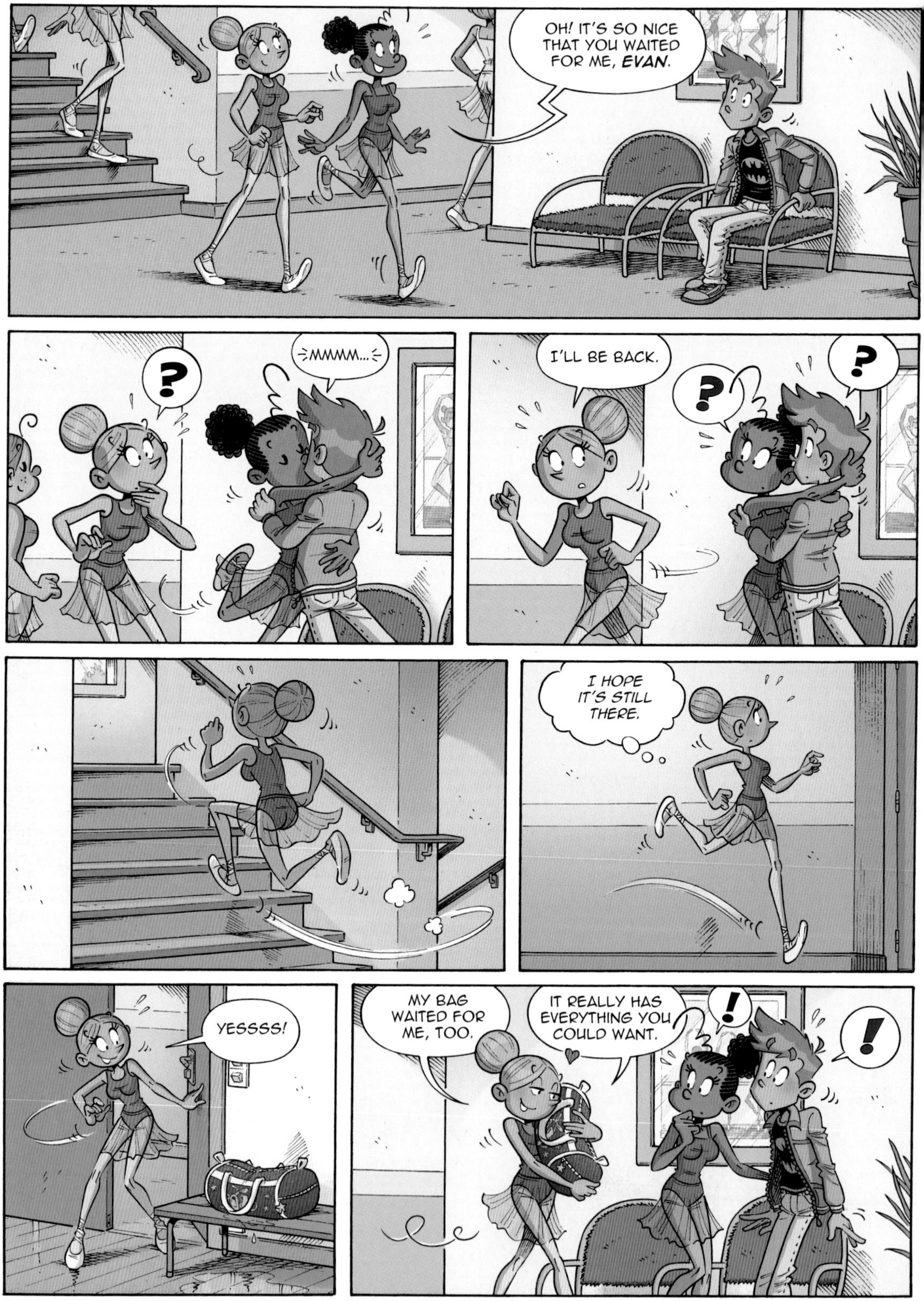
OH! IT'S SO NICE THAT YOU WAITED FOR ME, EVAN.
?
MMMMM...
I'LL BE BACK.
?
?
I HOPE IT'S STILL THERE.
YESSSS!
MY BAG WAITED FOR ME, TOO.
IT REALLY HAS EVERYTHING YOU COULD WANT.
!
!

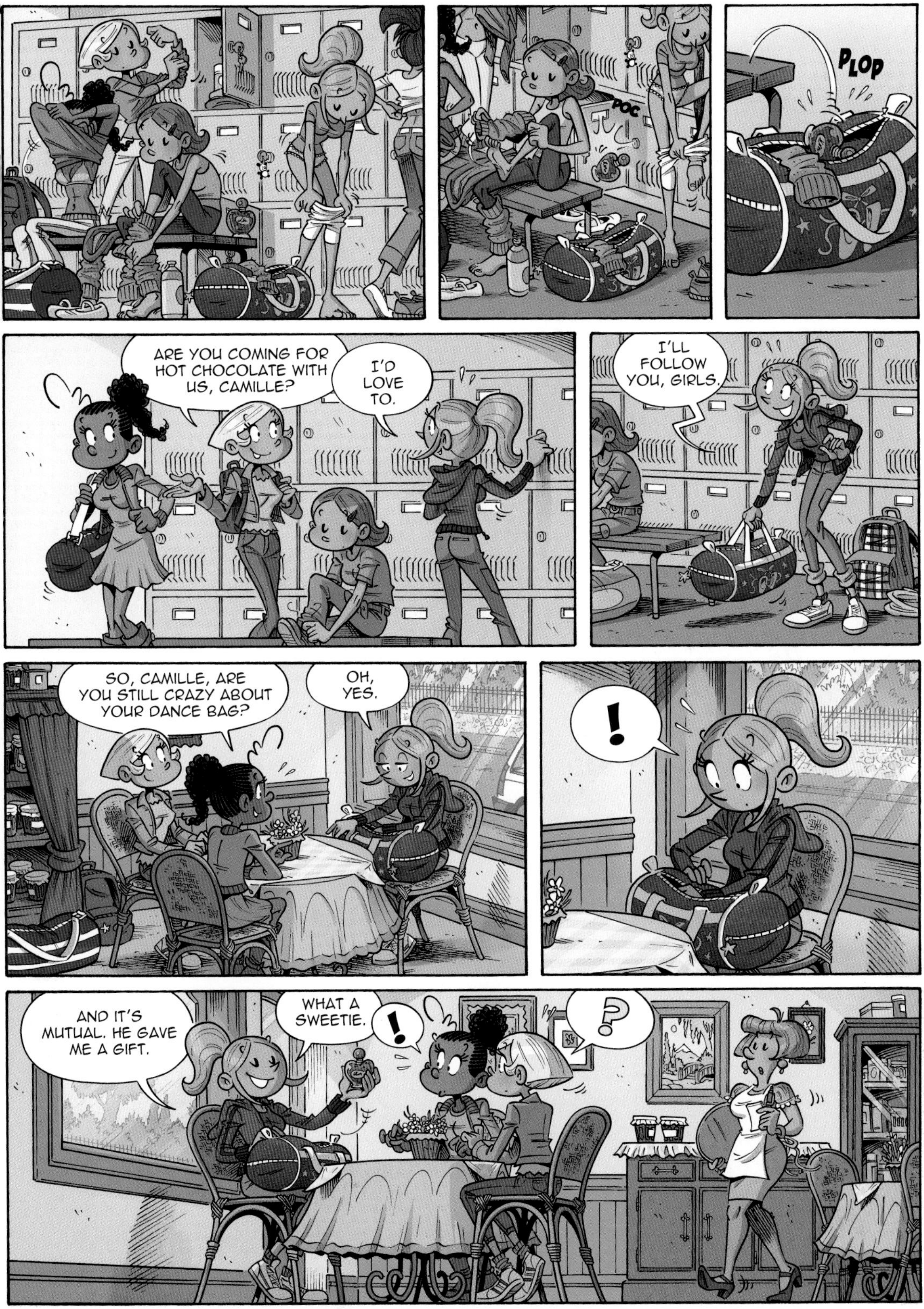
POC
PLOP
ARE YOU COMING FOR HOT CHOCOLATE WITH US, CAMILLE?
I'D LOVE TO.
I'LL FOLLOW YOU, GIRLS.
SO, CAMILLE, ARE YOU STILL CRAZY ABOUT YOUR DANCE BAG?
OH, YES.
!
AND IT'S MUTUAL. HE GAVE ME A GIFT.
WHAT A SWEETIE.
!
?

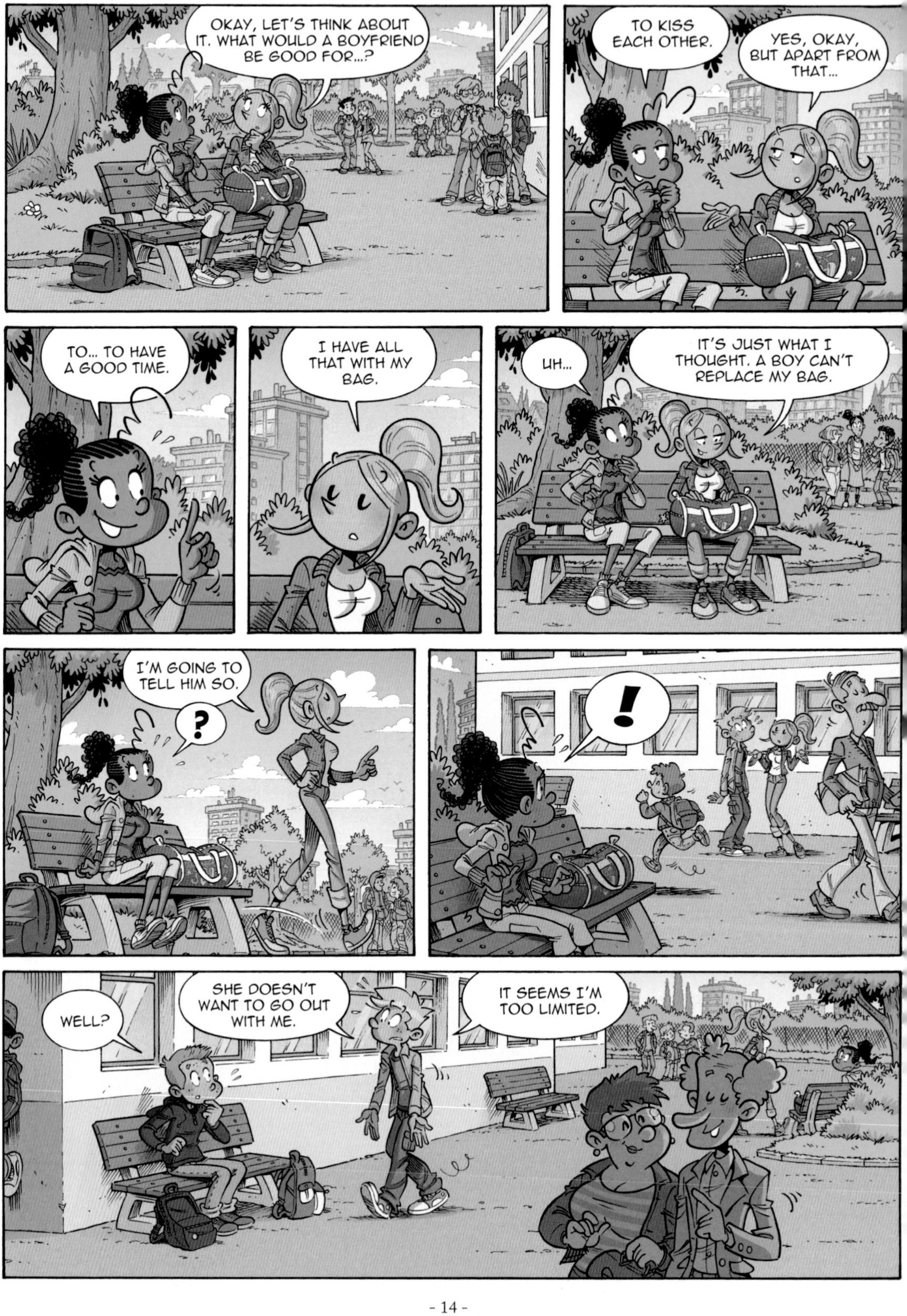
OKAY, LET'S THINK ABOUT IT. WHAT WOULD A BOYFRIEND BE GOOD FOR...?
TO KISS EACH OTHER.
YES, OKAY, BUT APART FROM THAT...
TO... TO HAVE A GOOD TIME.
I HAVE ALL THAT WITH MY BAG.
UH...
IT'S JUST WHAT I THOUGHT. A BOY CAN'T REPLACE MY BAG.
I'M GOING TO TELL HIM SO.
?
!
WELL?
SHE DOESN'T WANT TO GO OUT WITH ME.
IT SEEMS I'M TOO LIMITED.

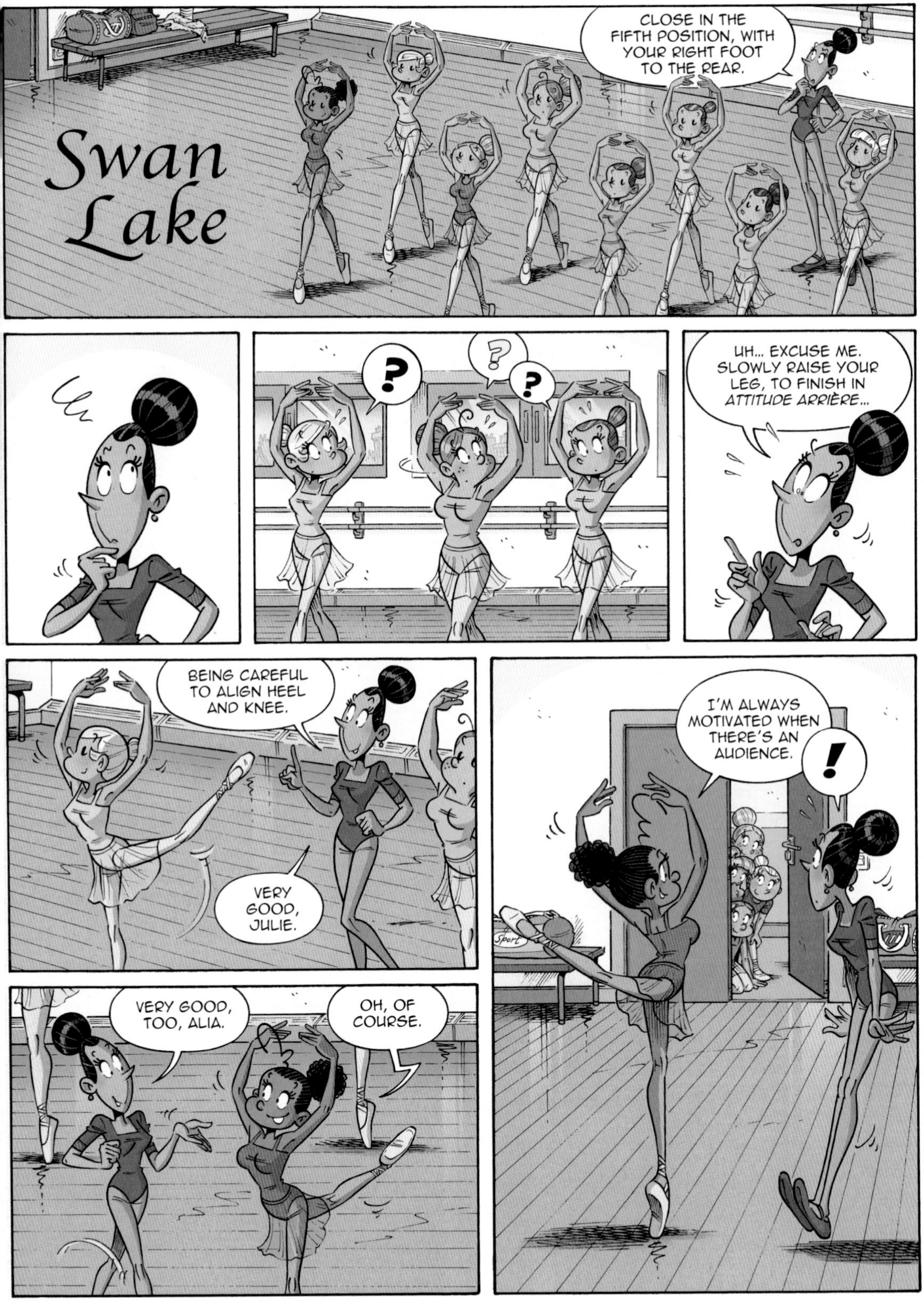
Swan Lake
CLOSE IN THE FIFTH POSITION, WITH YOUR RIGHT FOOT TO THE REAR.
?
?
?
UH... EXCUSE ME. SLOWLY RAISE YOUR LEG, TO FINISH IN ATTITUDE ARRIÈRE...
BEING CAREFUL TO ALIGN HEEL AND KNEE.
VERY GOOD, JULIE.
VERY GOOD, TOO, ALIA.
OH, OF COURSE.
I'M ALWAYS MOTIVATED WHEN THERE'S AN AUDIENCE.
!

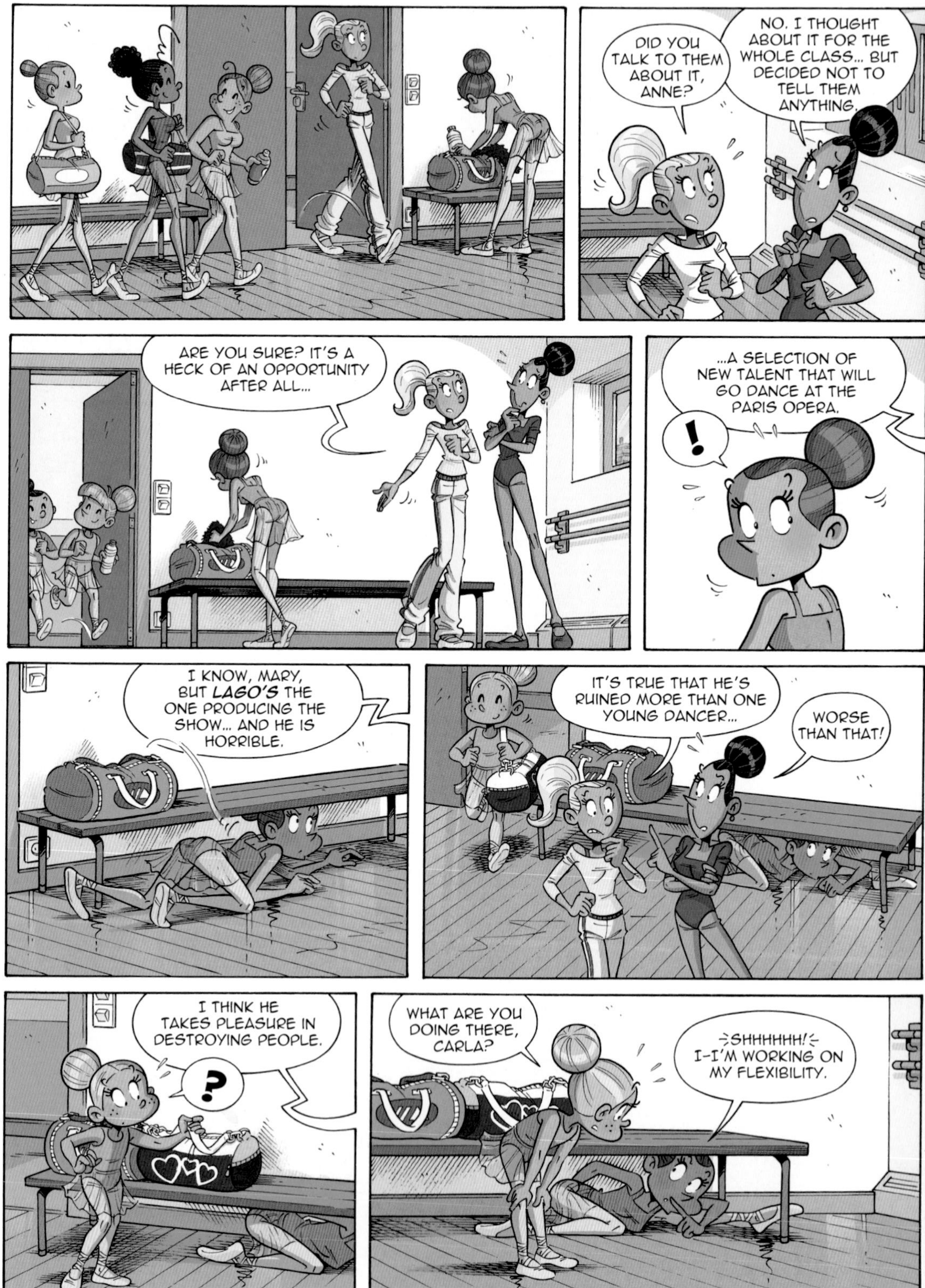
DID YOU TALK TO THEM ABOUT IT, ANNE?
NO. I THOUGHT ABOUT IT FOR THE WHOLE CLASS... BUT DECIDED NOT TO TELL THEM ANYTHING.
ARE YOU SURE? IT'S A HECK OF AN OPPORTUNITY AFTER ALL...
...A SELECTION OF NEW TALENT THAT WILL GO DANCE AT THE PARIS OPERA.
!
I KNOW, MARY, BUT LAGO'S THE ONE PRODUCING THE SHOW... AND HE IS HORRIBLE.
IT'S TRUE THAT HE'S RUINED MORE THAN ONE YOUNG DANCER...
WORSE THAN THAT!
I THINK HE TAKES PLEASURE IN DESTROYING PEOPLE.
?
WHAT ARE YOU DOING THERE, CARLA?
SHHHHHH! I-I'M WORKING ON MY FLEXIBILITY.

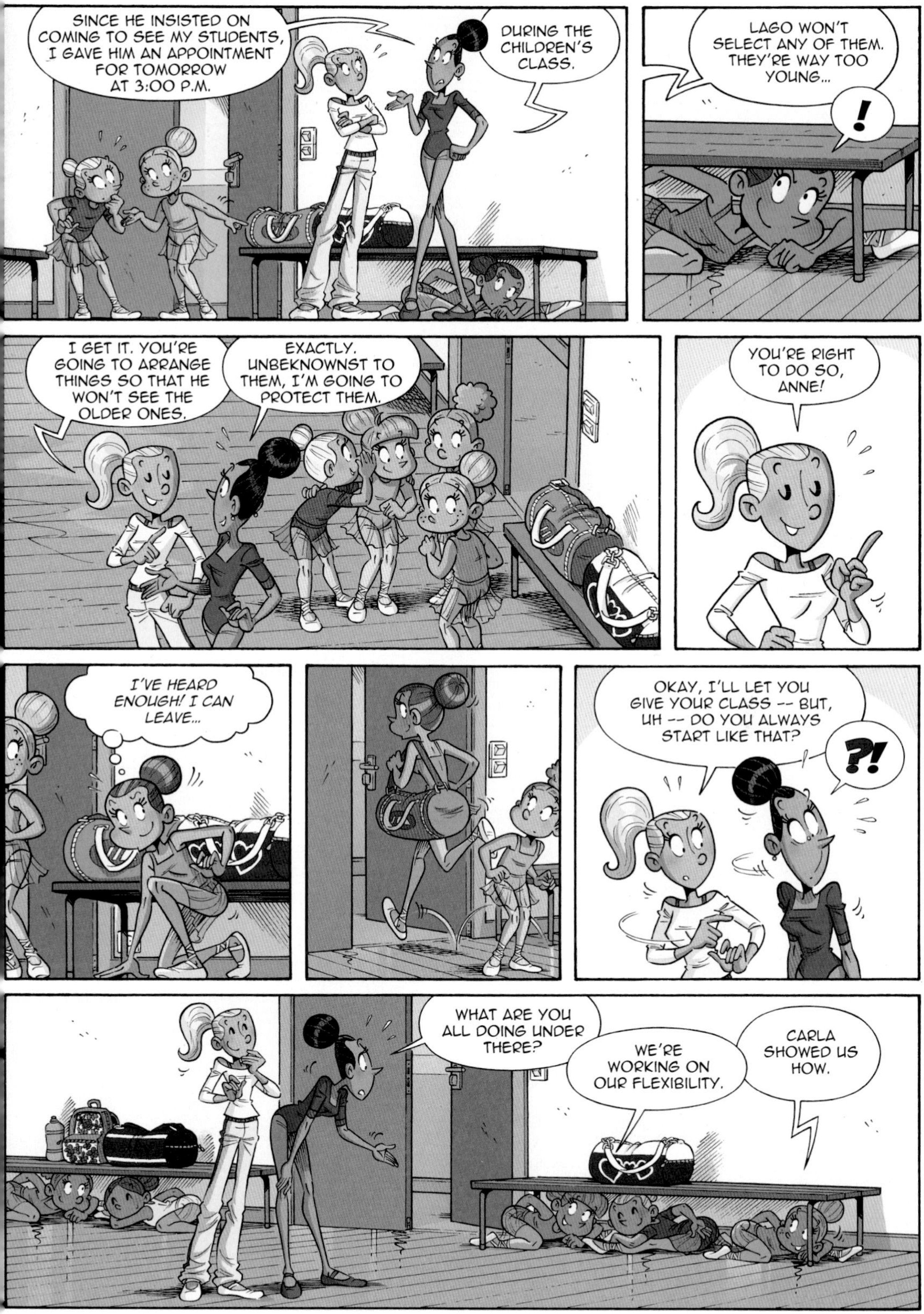
SINCE HE INSISTED ON COMING TO SEE MY STUDENTS, I GAVE HIM AN APPOINTMENT FOR TOMORROW AT 3:00 P.M.
DURING THE CHILDREN'S CLASS.
LAGO WON'T SELECT ANY OF THEM. THEY'RE WAY TOO YOUNG...
!
I GET IT. YOU'RE GOING TO ARRANGE THINGS SO THAT HE WON'T SEE THE OLDER ONES.
EXACTLY. UNBEKNOWNST TO THEM, I'M GOING TO PROTECT THEM.
YOU'RE RIGHT TO DO SO, ANNE!
I'VE HEARD ENOUGH! I CAN LEAVE...
OKAY, I'LL LET YOU GIVE YOUR CLASS -- BUT, UH -- DO YOU ALWAYS START LIKE THAT?
?!
WHAT ARE YOU ALL DOING UNDER THERE?
WE'RE WORKING ON OUR FLEXIBILITY.
CARLA SHOWED US HOW.

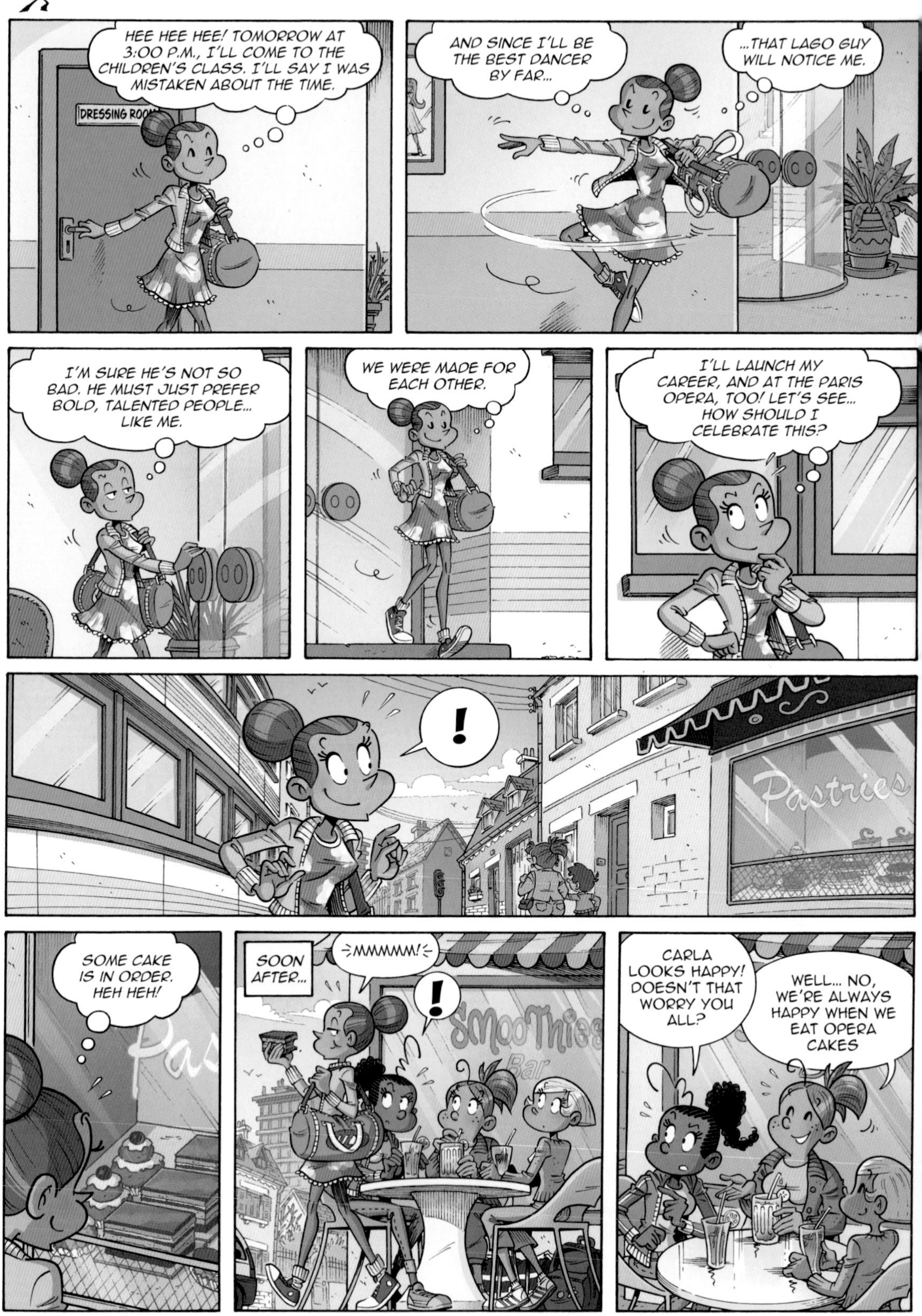
HEE HEE HEE! TOMORROW AT 3:00 P.M., I'LL COME TO THE CHILDREN'S CLASS. I'LL SAY I WAS MISTAKEN ABOUT THE TIME.
DRESSING ROOM
AND SINCE I'LL BE THE BEST DANCER BY FAR...
...THAT LAGO GUY WILL NOTICE ME.
I'M SURE HE'S NOT SO BAD. HE MUST JUST PREFER BOLD, TALENTED PEOPLE... LIKE ME.
WE WERE MADE FOR EACH OTHER.
I'LL LAUNCH MY CAREER, AND AT THE PARIS OPERA, TOO! LET'S SEE... HOW SHOULD I CELEBRATE THIS?
!
Pastries
SOME CAKE IS IN ORDER. HEH HEH!
SOON AFTER...
MMMMMM!
!
SmooThies Bar
CARLA LOOKS HAPPY! DOESN'T THAT WORRY YOU ALL?
WELL... NO, WE'RE ALWAYS HAPPY WHEN WE EAT OPERA CAKES

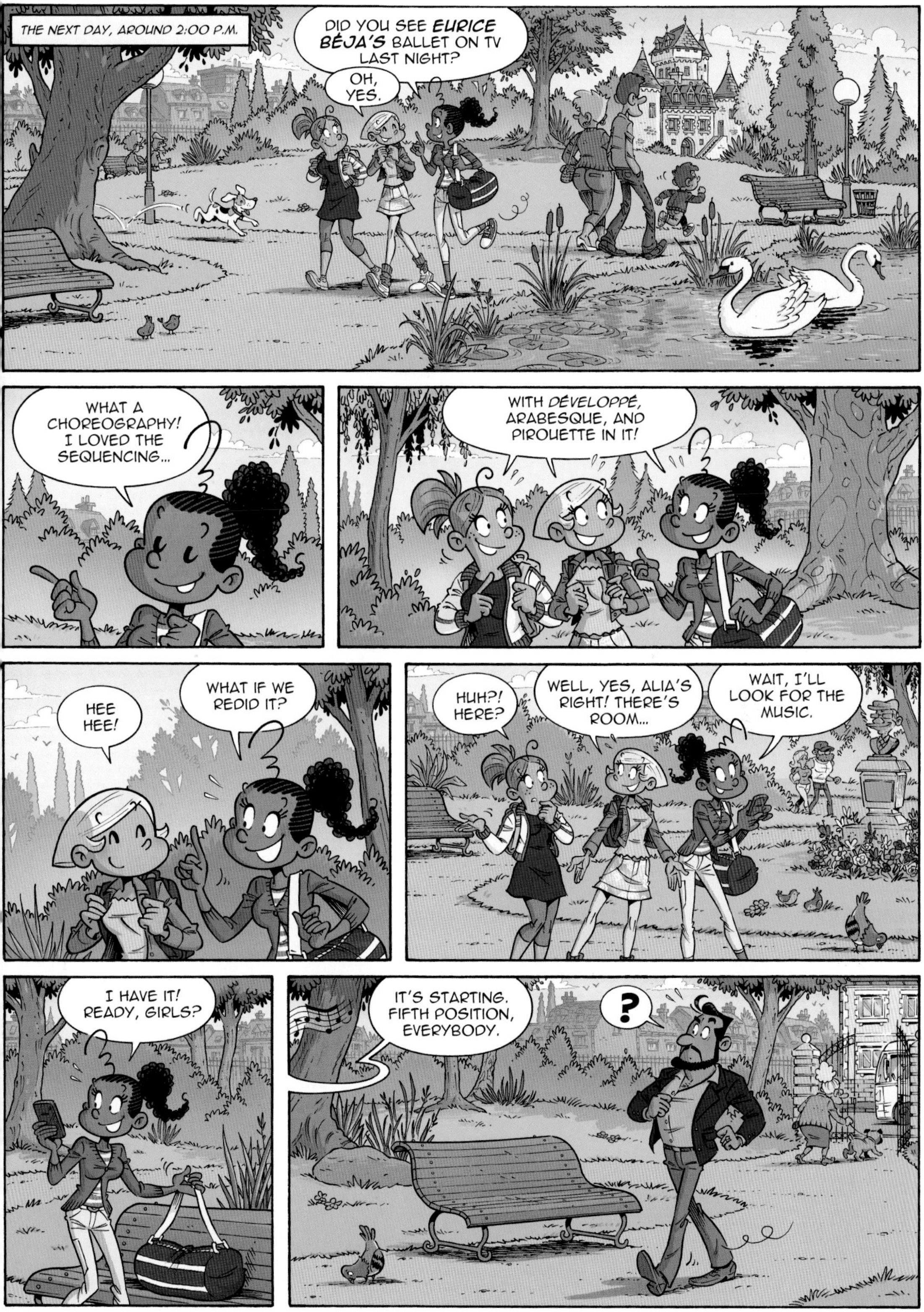
THE NEXT DAY, AROUND 2:00 P.M.
DID YOU SEE EURICE BÉJA'S BALLET ON TV LAST NIGHT?
OH, YES.
WHAT A CHOREOGRAPHY! I LOVED THE SEQUENCING...
WITH DÉVELOPPÉ, ARABESQUE, AND PIROUETTE IN IT!
HEE HEE!
WHAT IF WE REDID IT?
HUH?! HERE?
WELL, YES, ALIA'S RIGHT! THERE'S ROOM...
WAIT, I'LL LOOK FOR THE MUSIC.
I HAVE IT! READY, GIRLS?
IT'S STARTING. FIFTH POSITION, EVERYBODY.
?

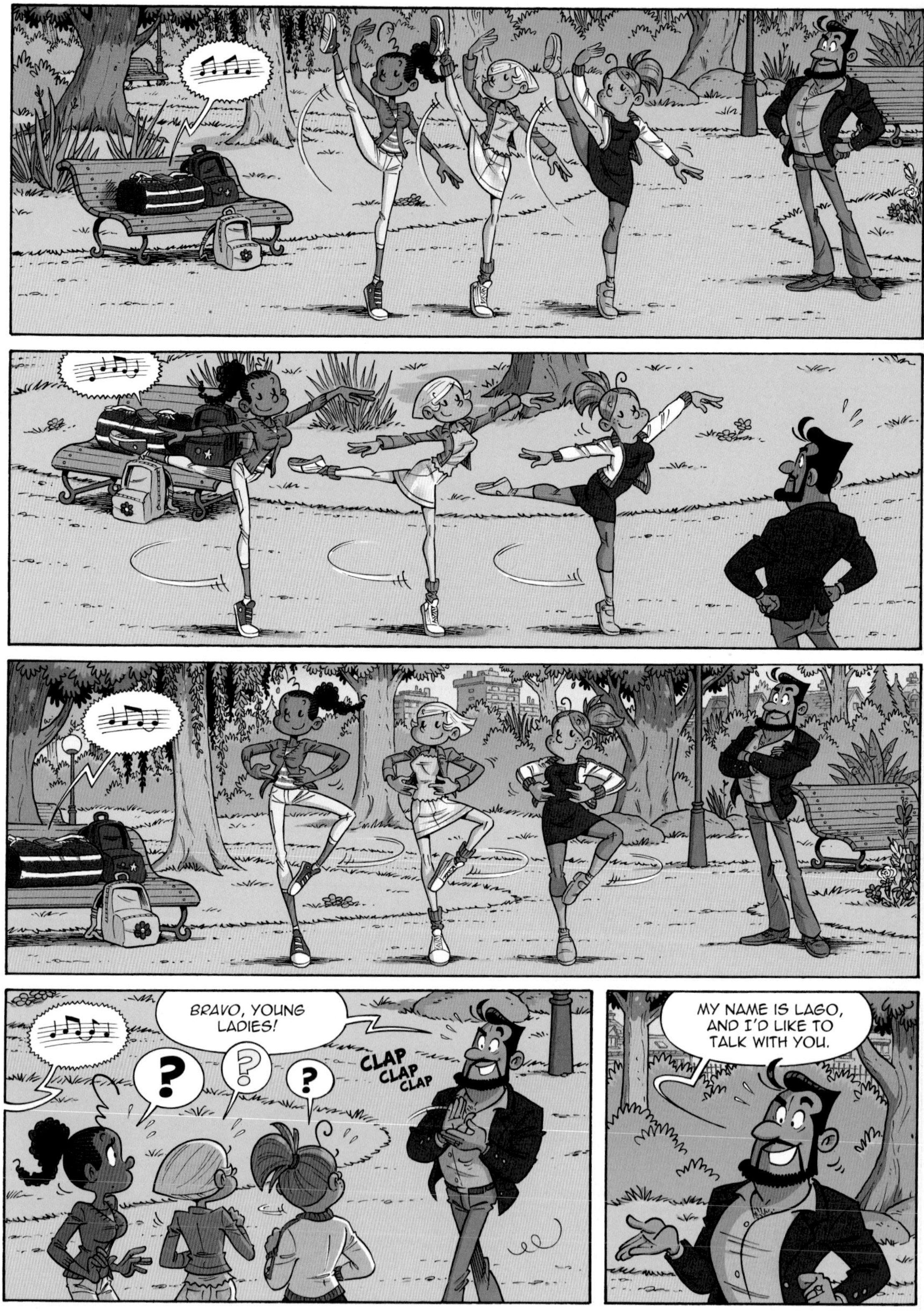
BRAVO, YOUNG LADIES!
?
?
?
CLAP CLAP CLAP
MY NAME IS LAGO, AND I'D LIKE TO TALK WITH YOU.

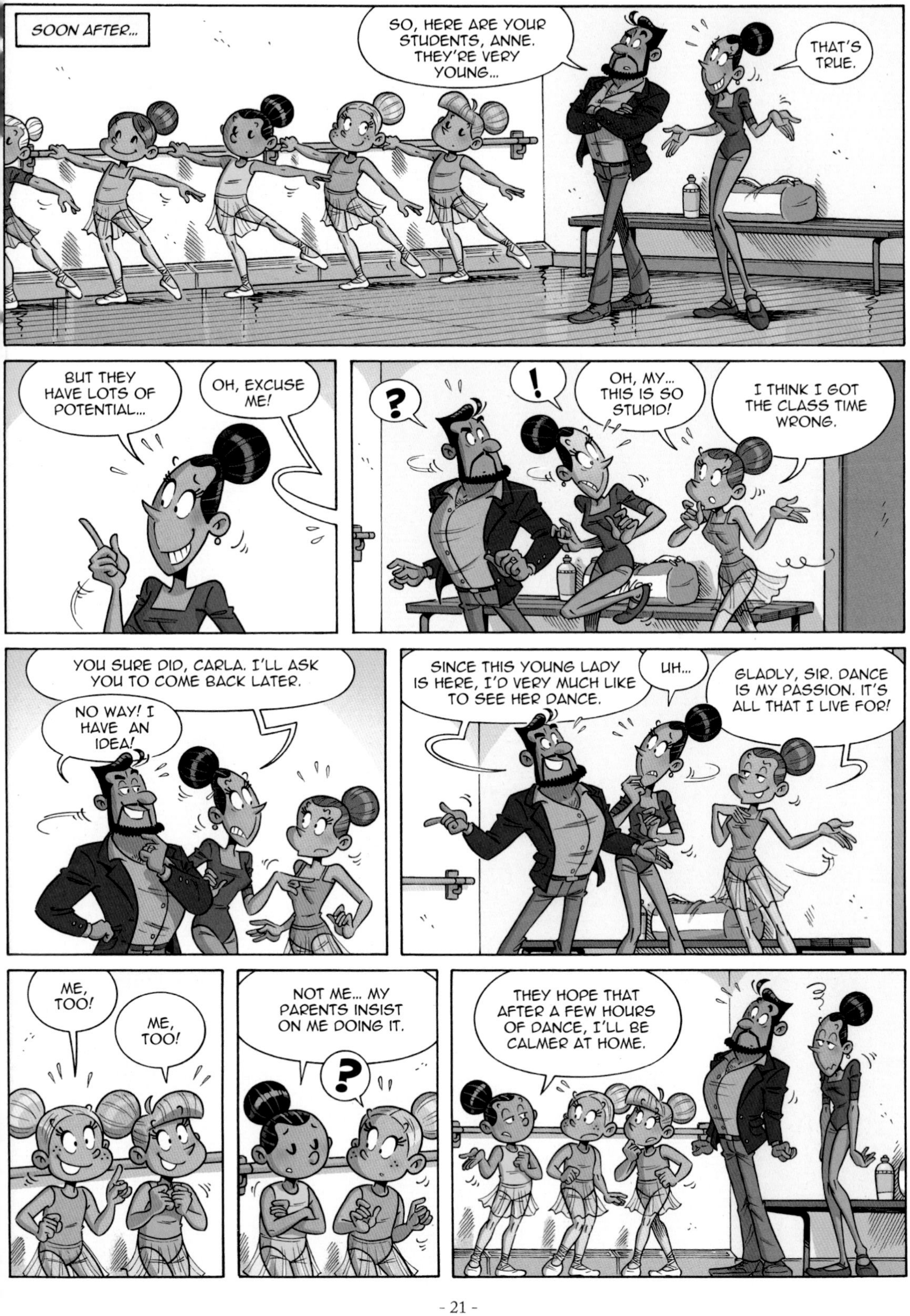
SOON AFTER...
SO, HERE ARE YOUR STUDENTS, ANNE. THEY'RE VERY YOUNG...
THAT'S TRUE.
BUT THEY HAVE LOTS OF POTENTIAL...
OH, EXCUSE ME!
?
!
OH, MY... THIS IS SO STUPID!
I THINK I GOT THE CLASS TIME WRONG.
YOU SURE DID, CARLA. I'LL ASK YOU TO COME BACK LATER.
NO WAY! I HAVE AN IDEA!
SINCE THIS YOUNG LADY IS HERE, I'D VERY MUCH LIKE TO SEE HER DANCE.
UH...
GLADLY, SIR. DANCE IS MY PASSION. IT'S ALL THAT I LIVE FOR!
ME, TOO!
ME, TOO!
NOT ME... MY PARENTS INSIST ON ME DOING IT.
?
THEY HOPE THAT AFTER A FEW HOURS OF DANCE, I'LL BE CALMER AT HOME.

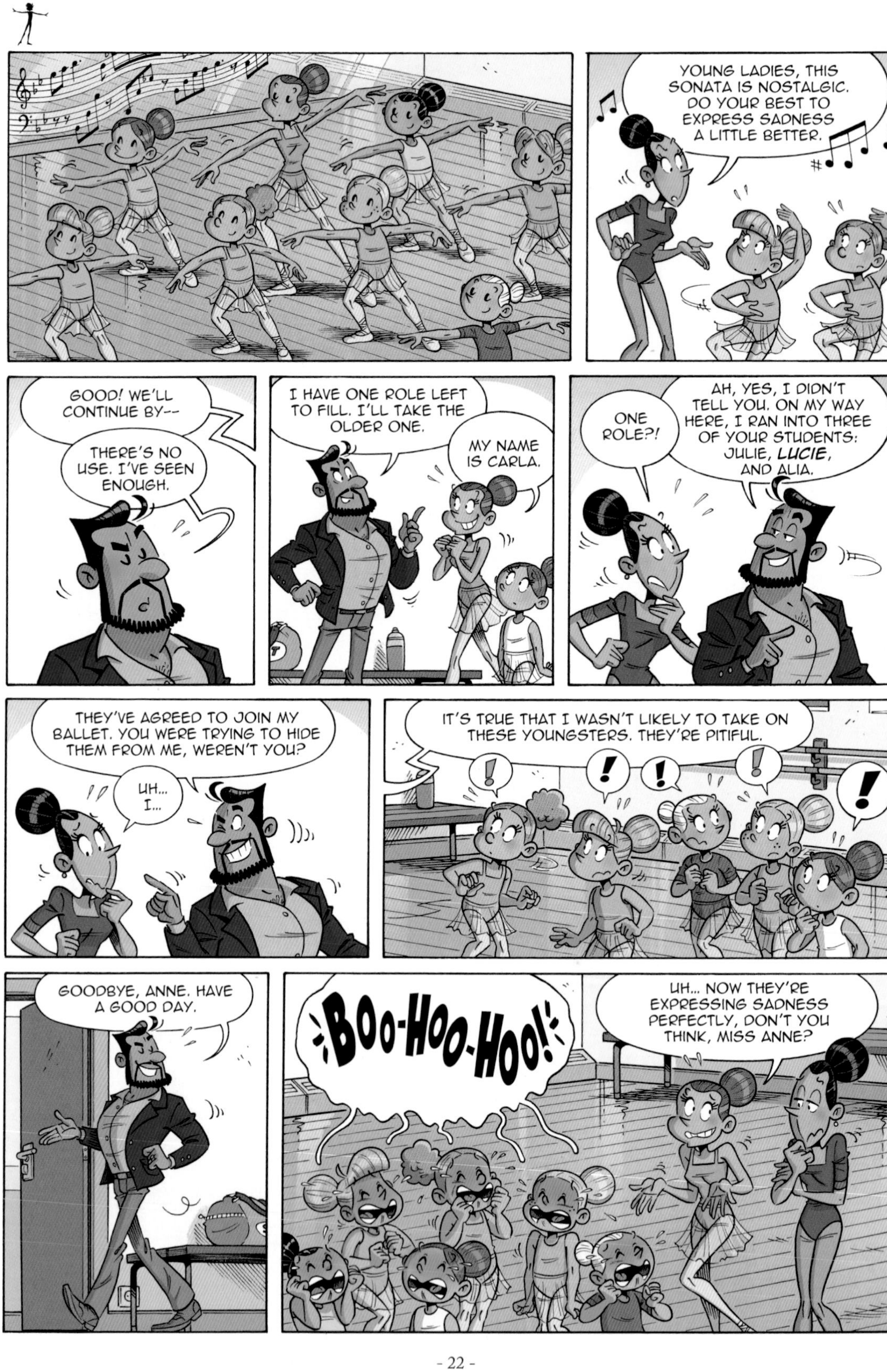
YOUNG LADIES, THIS SONATA IS NOSTALGIC. DO YOUR BEST TO EXPRESS SADNESS A LITTLE BETTER.
GOOD! WE'LL CONTINUE BY--
THERE'S NO USE. I'VE SEEN ENOUGH.
I HAVE ONE ROLE LEFT TO FILL. I'LL TAKE THE OLDER ONE.
MY NAME IS CARLA.
ONE ROLE?!
AH, YES, I DIDN'T TELL YOU. ON MY WAY HERE, I RAN INTO THREE OF YOUR STUDENTS: JULIE, ***LUCIE***, AND ALIA.
THEY'VE AGREED TO JOIN MY BALLET. YOU WERE TRYING TO HIDE THEM FROM ME, WEREN'T YOU?
UH... I...
IT'S TRUE THAT I WASN'T LIKELY TO TAKE ON THESE YOUNGSTERS. THEY'RE PITIFUL.
!
!
!
!
!
GOODBYE, ANNE. HAVE A GOOD DAY.
BOO-HOO-HOO!
UH... NOW THEY'RE EXPRESSING SADNESS PERFECTLY, DON'T YOU THINK, MISS ANNE?

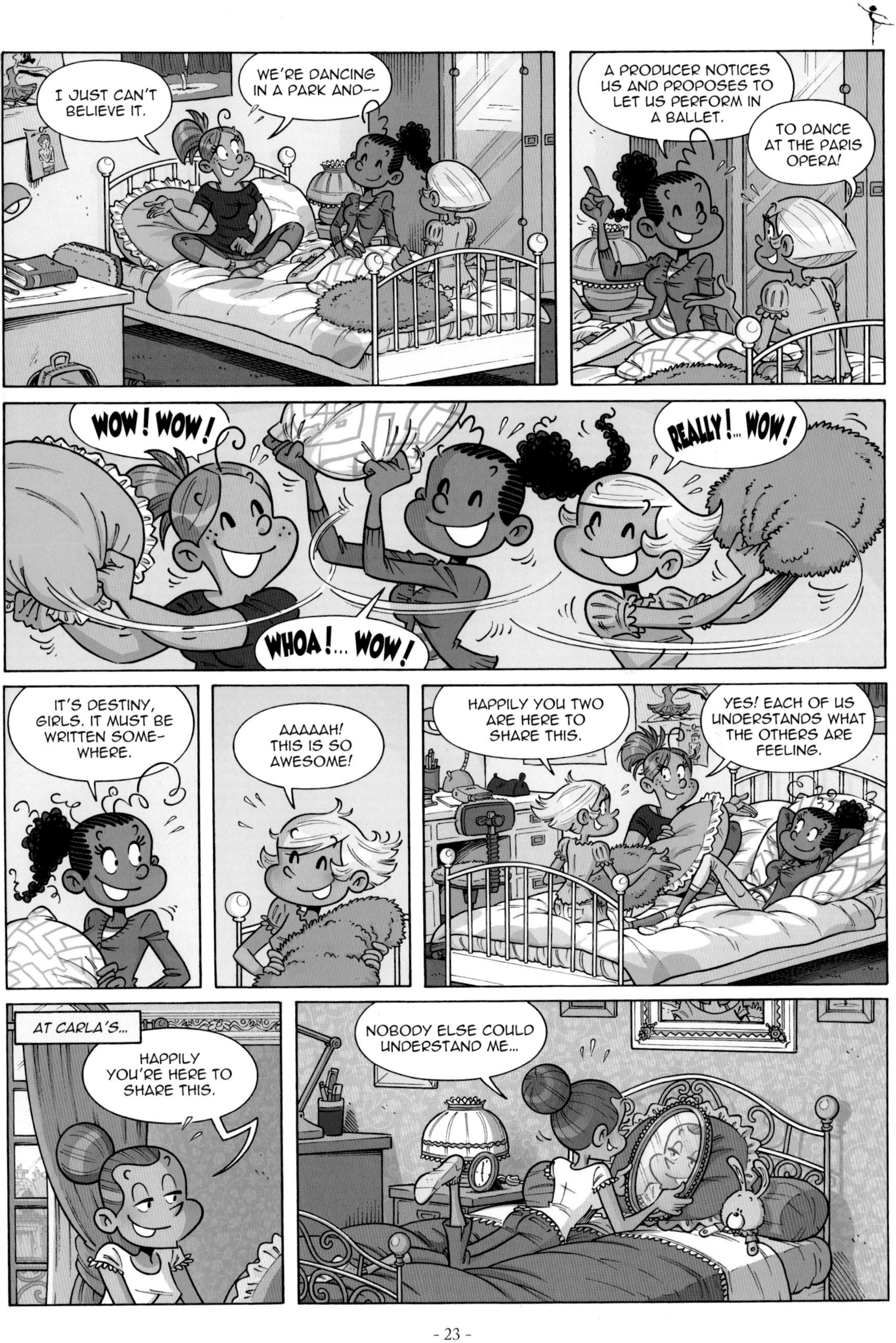
I JUST CAN'T BELIEVE IT.
WE'RE DANCING IN A PARK AND--
A PRODUCER NOTICES US AND PROPOSES TO LET US PERFORM IN A BALLET.
TO DANCE AT THE PARIS OPERA!
WOW! WOW!
WHOA!... WOW!
REALLY!... WOW!
IT'S DESTINY, GIRLS. IT MUST BE WRITTEN SOME-WHERE.
AAAAAH! THIS IS SO AWESOME!
HAPPILY YOU TWO ARE HERE TO SHARE THIS.
YES! EACH OF US UNDERSTANDS WHAT THE OTHERS ARE FEELING.
AT CARLA'S...
HAPPILY YOU'RE HERE TO SHARE THIS.
NOBODY ELSE COULD UNDERSTAND ME...

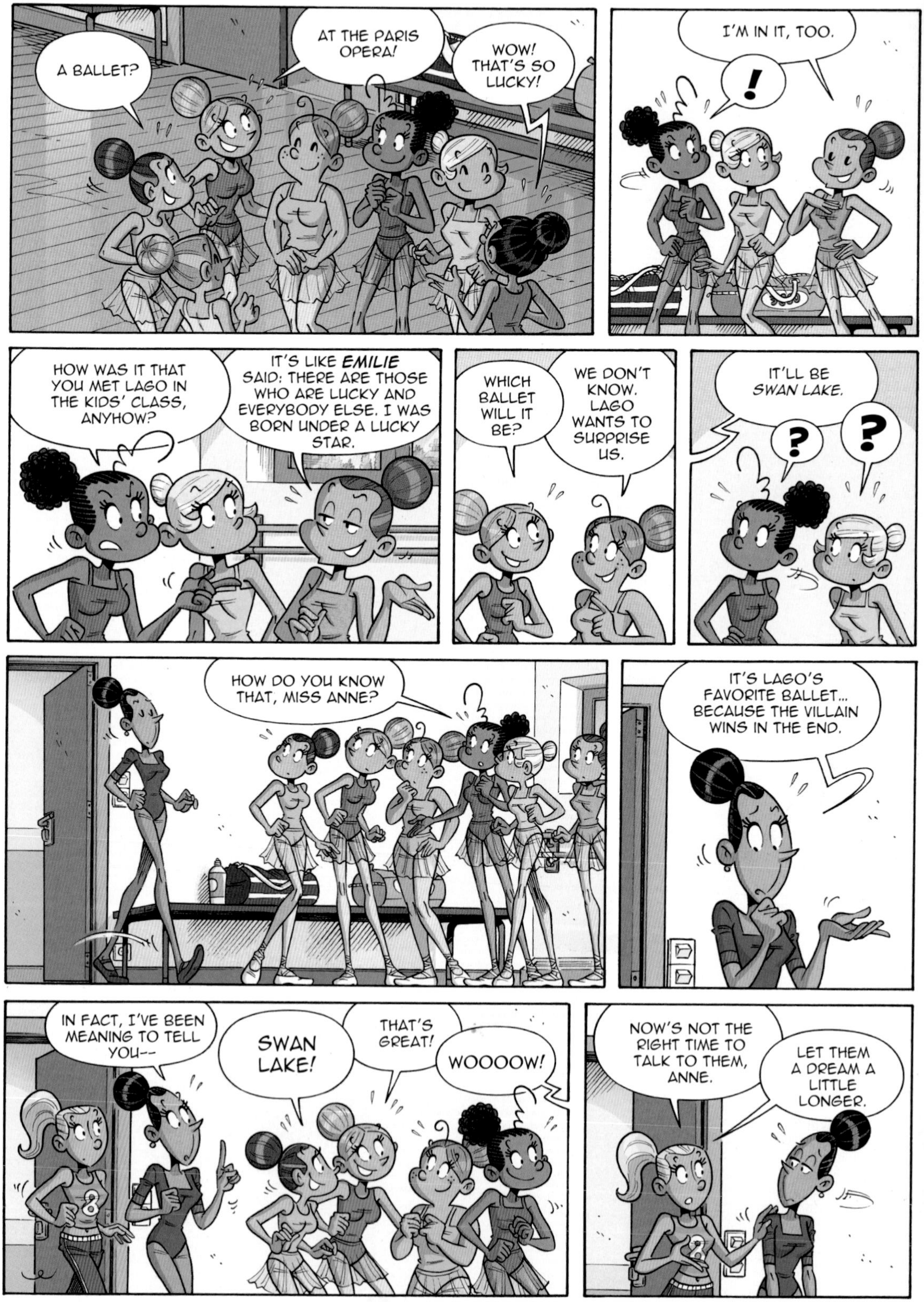
A BALLET?
AT THE PARIS OPERA!
WOW! THAT'S SO LUCKY!
I'M IN IT, TOO.
!
HOW WAS IT THAT YOU MET LAGO IN THE KIDS' CLASS, ANYHOW?
IT'S LIKE **EMILIE** SAID: THERE ARE THOSE WHO ARE LUCKY AND EVERYBODY ELSE. I WAS BORN UNDER A LUCKY STAR.
WHICH BALLET WILL IT BE?
WE DON'T KNOW. LAGO WANTS TO SURPRISE US.
IT'LL BE *SWAN LAKE.*
?
?
HOW DO YOU KNOW THAT, MISS ANNE?
IT'S LAGO'S FAVORITE BALLET... BECAUSE THE VILLAIN WINS IN THE END.
IN FACT, I'VE BEEN MEANING TO TELL YOU--
SWAN LAKE!
THAT'S GREAT!
WOOOOW!
NOW'S NOT THE RIGHT TIME TO TALK TO THEM, ANNE.
LET THEM A DREAM A LITTLE LONGER.

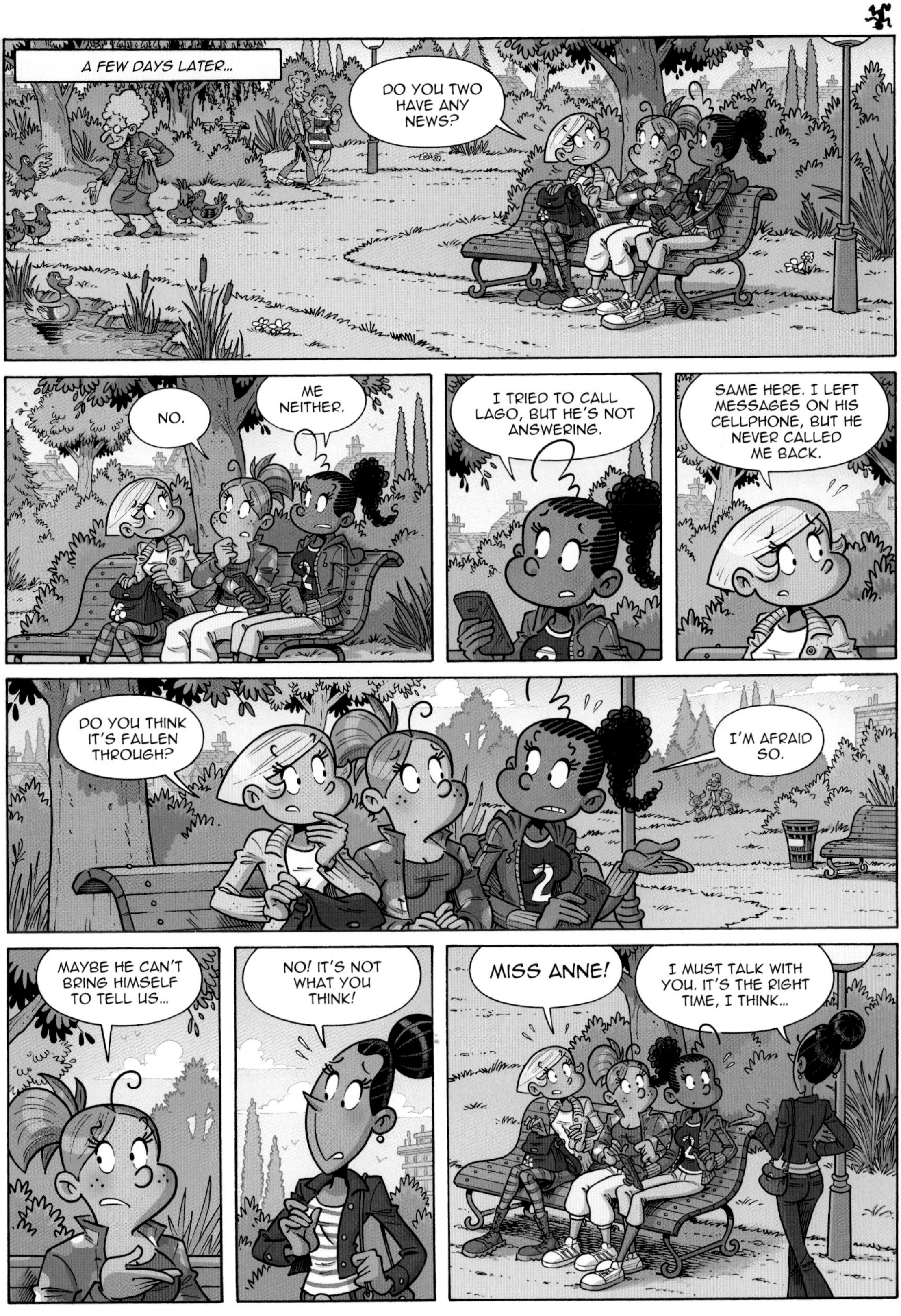
A FEW DAYS LATER...
DO YOU TWO HAVE ANY NEWS?
NO.
ME NEITHER.
I TRIED TO CALL LAGO, BUT HE'S NOT ANSWERING.
SAME HERE. I LEFT MESSAGES ON HIS CELLPHONE, BUT HE NEVER CALLED ME BACK.
DO YOU THINK IT'S FALLEN THROUGH?
I'M AFRAID SO.
MAYBE HE CAN'T BRING HIMSELF TO TELL US...
NO! IT'S NOT WHAT YOU THINK!
MISS ANNE!
I MUST TALK WITH YOU. IT'S THE RIGHT TIME, I THINK...

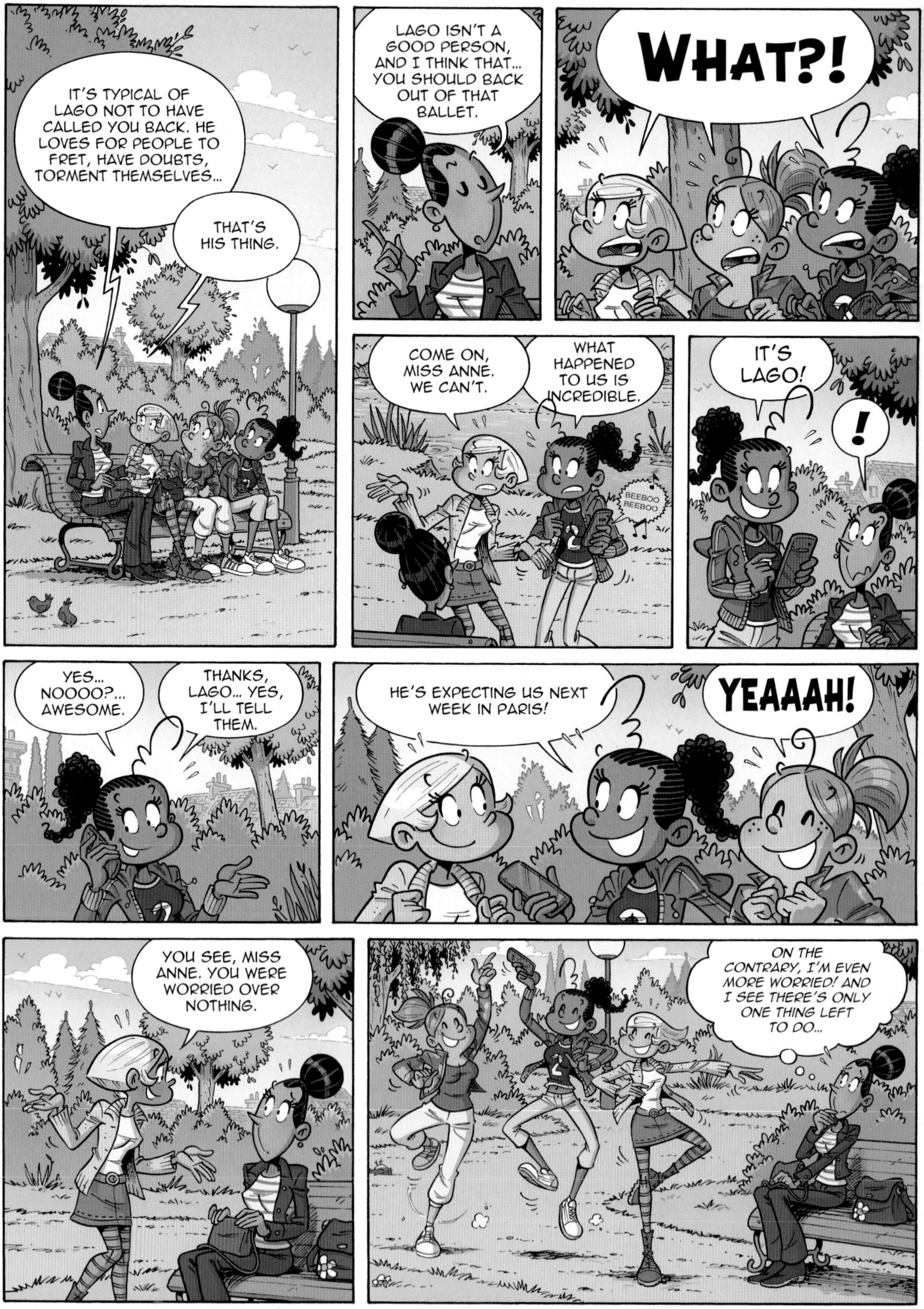

IT'S TYPICAL OF LAGO NOT TO HAVE CALLED YOU BACK. HE LOVES FOR PEOPLE TO FRET, HAVE DOUBTS, TORMENT THEMSELVES...
THAT'S HIS THING.
LAGO ISN'T A GOOD PERSON, AND I THINK THAT... YOU SHOULD BACK OUT OF THAT BALLET.
WHAT?!
COME ON, MISS ANNE. WE CAN'T.
WHAT HAPPENED TO US IS INCREDIBLE.
BEEBOO BEEBOO
IT'S LAGO!
!
YES... NOOOO?... AWESOME.
THANKS, LAGO... YES, I'LL TELL THEM.
HE'S EXPECTING US NEXT WEEK IN PARIS!
YEAAAH!
YOU SEE, MISS ANNE. YOU WERE WORRIED OVER NOTHING.
ON THE CONTRARY, I'M EVEN MORE WORRIED! AND I SEE THERE'S ONLY ONE THING LEFT TO DO...

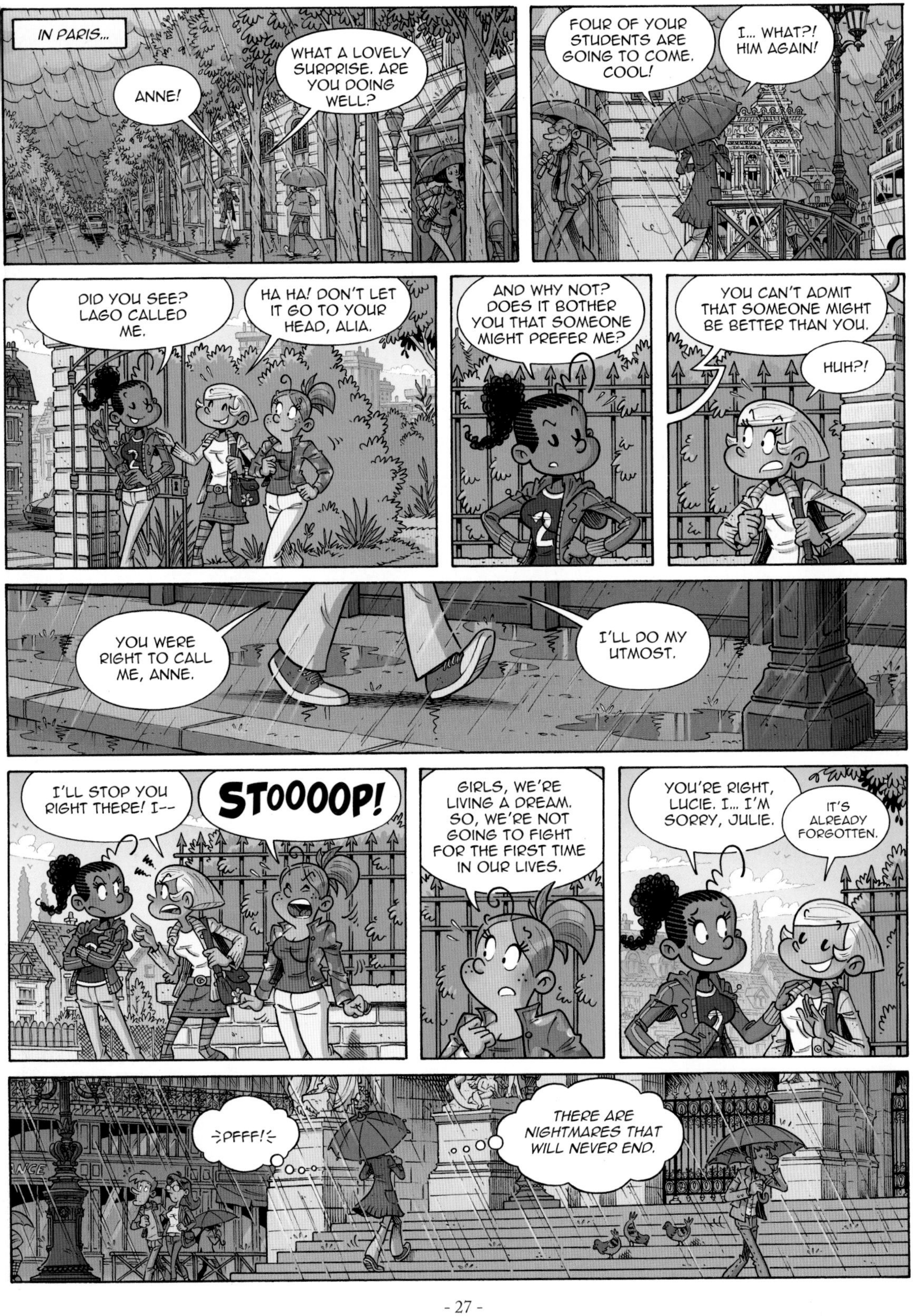
IN PARIS...
ANNE!
WHAT A LOVELY SURPRISE. ARE YOU DOING WELL?
FOUR OF YOUR STUDENTS ARE GOING TO COME. COOL!
I... WHAT?! HIM AGAIN!
DID YOU SEE? LAGO CALLED ME.
HA HA! DON'T LET IT GO TO YOUR HEAD, ALIA.
AND WHY NOT? DOES IT BOTHER YOU THAT SOMEONE MIGHT PREFER ME?
YOU CAN'T ADMIT THAT SOMEONE MIGHT BE BETTER THAN YOU.
HUH?!
YOU WERE RIGHT TO CALL ME, ANNE.
I'LL DO MY UTMOST.
I'LL STOP YOU RIGHT THERE! I--
STOOOOP!
GIRLS, WE'RE LIVING A DREAM. SO, WE'RE NOT GOING TO FIGHT FOR THE FIRST TIME IN OUR LIVES.
YOU'RE RIGHT, LUCIE. I... I'M SORRY, JULIE.
IT'S ALREADY FORGOTTEN.
PFFF!
THERE ARE NIGHTMARES THAT WILL NEVER END.

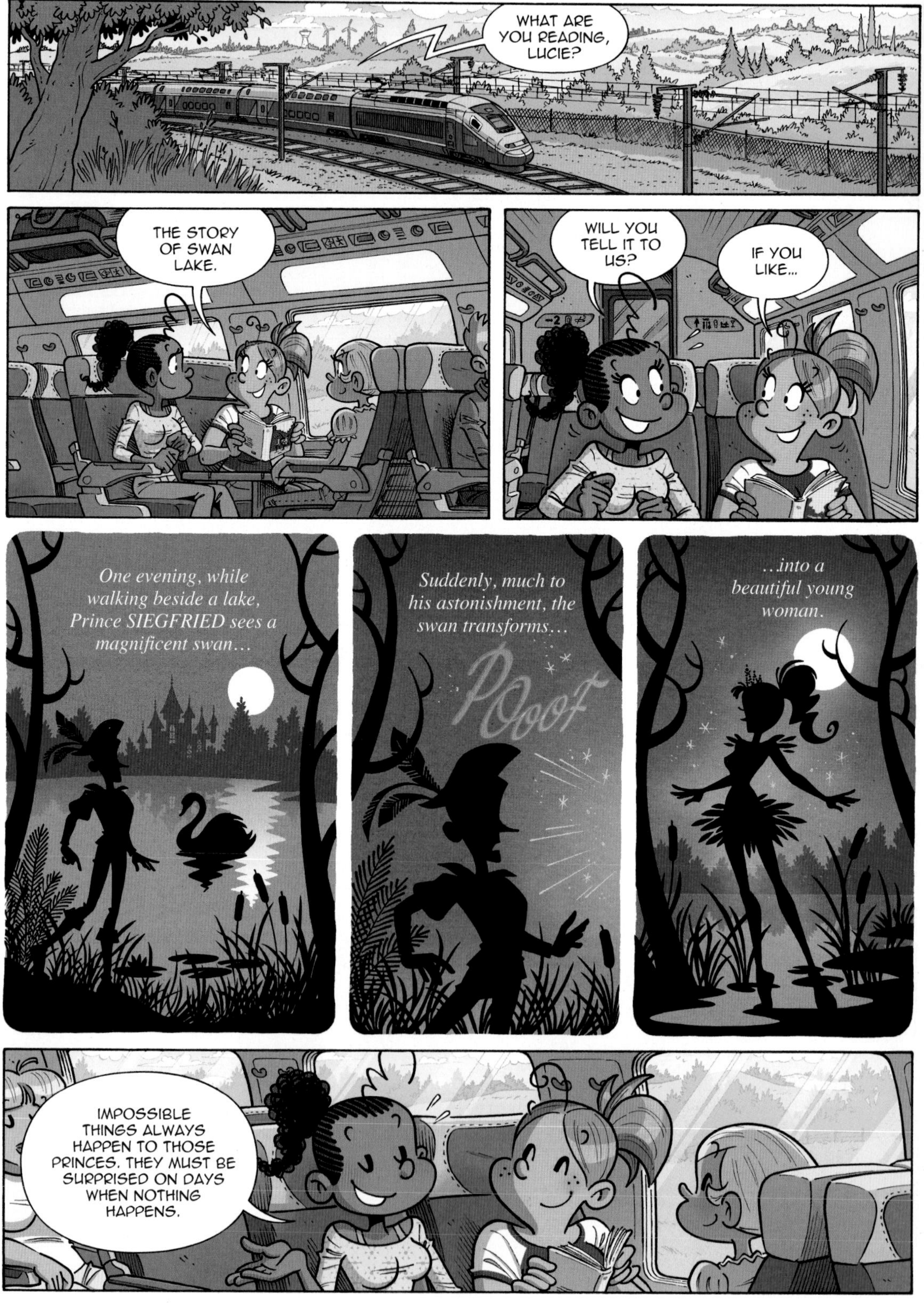
WHAT ARE YOU READING, LUCIE?
THE STORY OF SWAN LAKE.
WILL YOU TELL IT TO US?
IF YOU LIKE...
One evening, while walking beside a lake, Prince SIEGFRIED sees a magnificent swan…
Suddenly, much to his astonishment, the swan transforms…
POOOF
…into a beautiful young woman.
IMPOSSIBLE THINGS ALWAYS HAPPEN TO THOSE PRINCES. THEY MUST BE SURPRISED ON DAYS WHEN NOTHING HAPPENS.

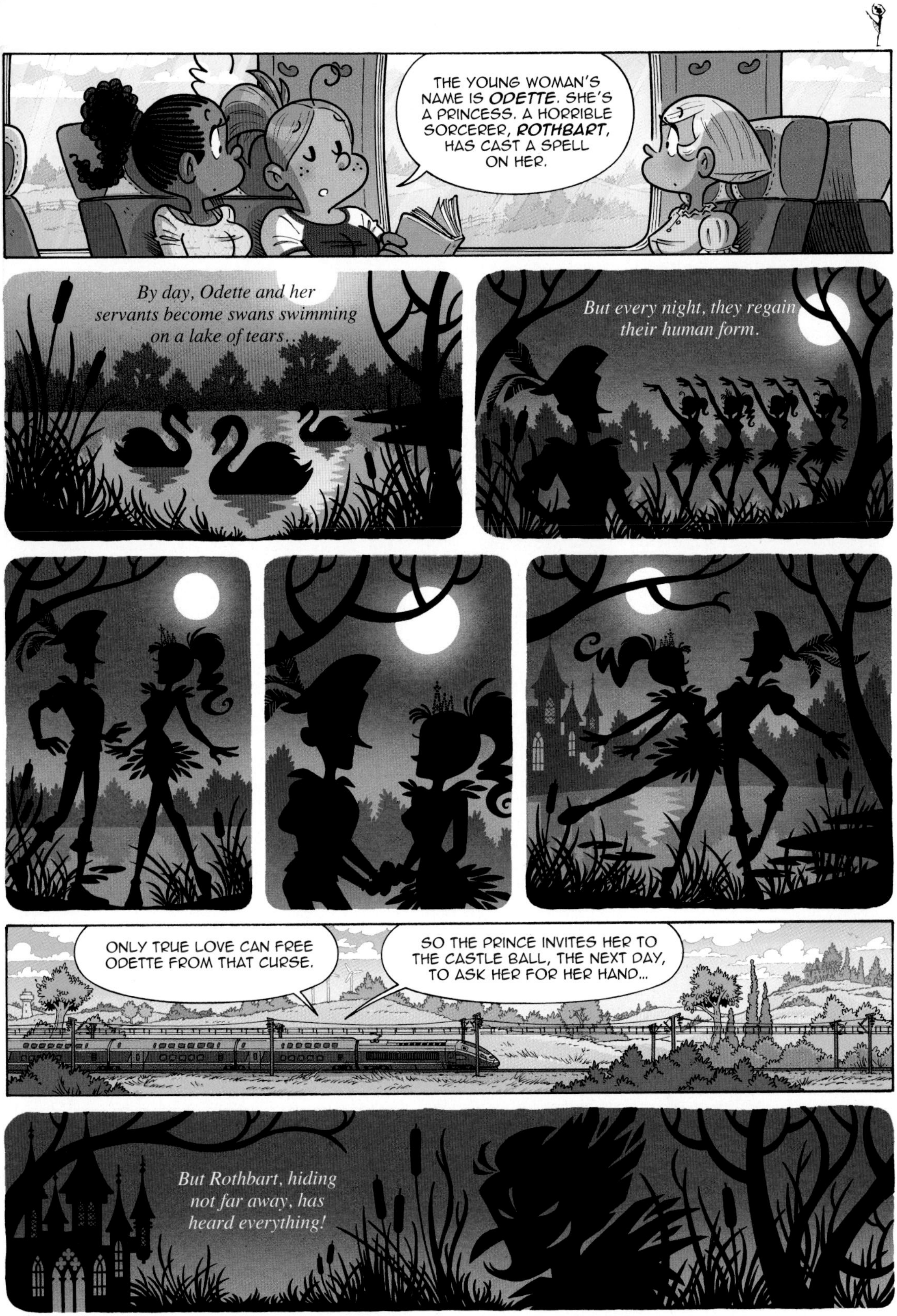
THE YOUNG WOMAN'S NAME IS ODETTE. SHE'S A PRINCESS. A HORRIBLE SORCERER, ROTHBART, HAS CAST A SPELL ON HER.
By day, Odette and her servants become swans swimming on a lake of tears...
But every night, they regain their human form.
ONLY TRUE LOVE CAN FREE ODETTE FROM THAT CURSE.
SO THE PRINCE INVITES HER TO THE CASTLE BALL, THE NEXT DAY, TO ASK HER FOR HER HAND...
But Rothbart, hiding not far away, has heard everything!

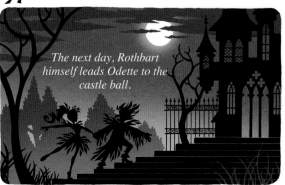

The next day, Rothbart himself leads Odette to the castle ball.

But Odette is acting strange, as though transformed…

It's because it's not Odette, but ODILE, the evil mage's daughter.

Siegfried, however, keeps his promise and swears eternal love to her.

That's when the real Odette arrives.

And once she realizes what's happened, she runs away and, despairing, throws herself into the lake.

Siegfried follows her… He dives in to save her.

But they both drown.

THEIR SOULS MEET AGAIN IN DEATH AND, SINCE THEY LOVE ONE ANOTHER, THE CURSE IS LIFTED FOR THE OTHER SWANS.

THAT'S SO BEAUTIFUL.

AND SO SAD...

I SURE HOPE THAT'S THE BALLET WE'LL BE DANCING.

HMM... I DON'T KNOW WHY, BUT SOMETHING'S TELLING ME YES.

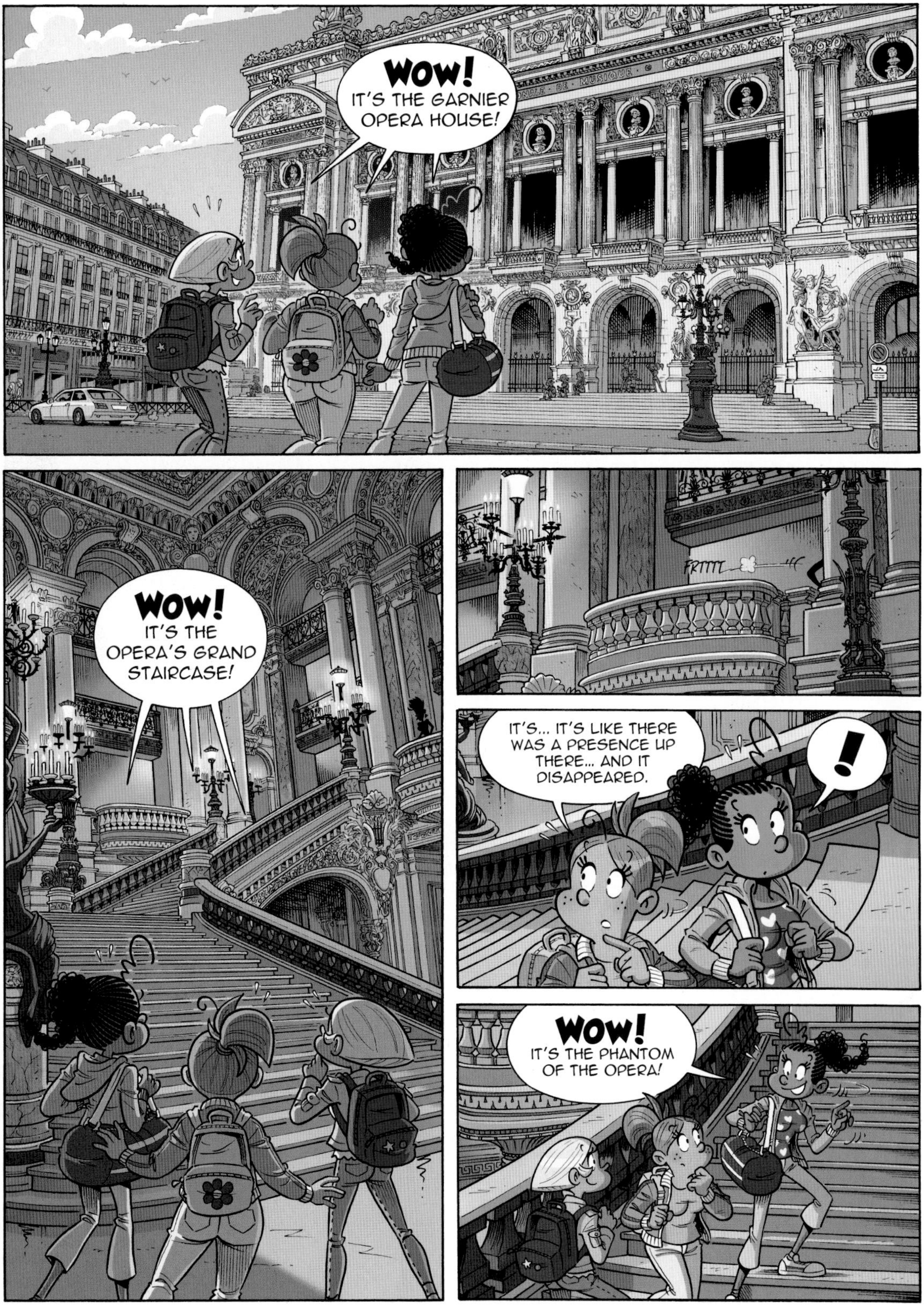
WOW! IT'S THE GARNIER OPERA HOUSE!
WOW! IT'S THE OPERA'S GRAND STAIRCASE!
FRTTTT
IT'S... IT'S LIKE THERE WAS A PRESENCE UP THERE... AND IT DISAPPEARED.
!
WOW! IT'S THE PHANTOM OF THE OPERA!

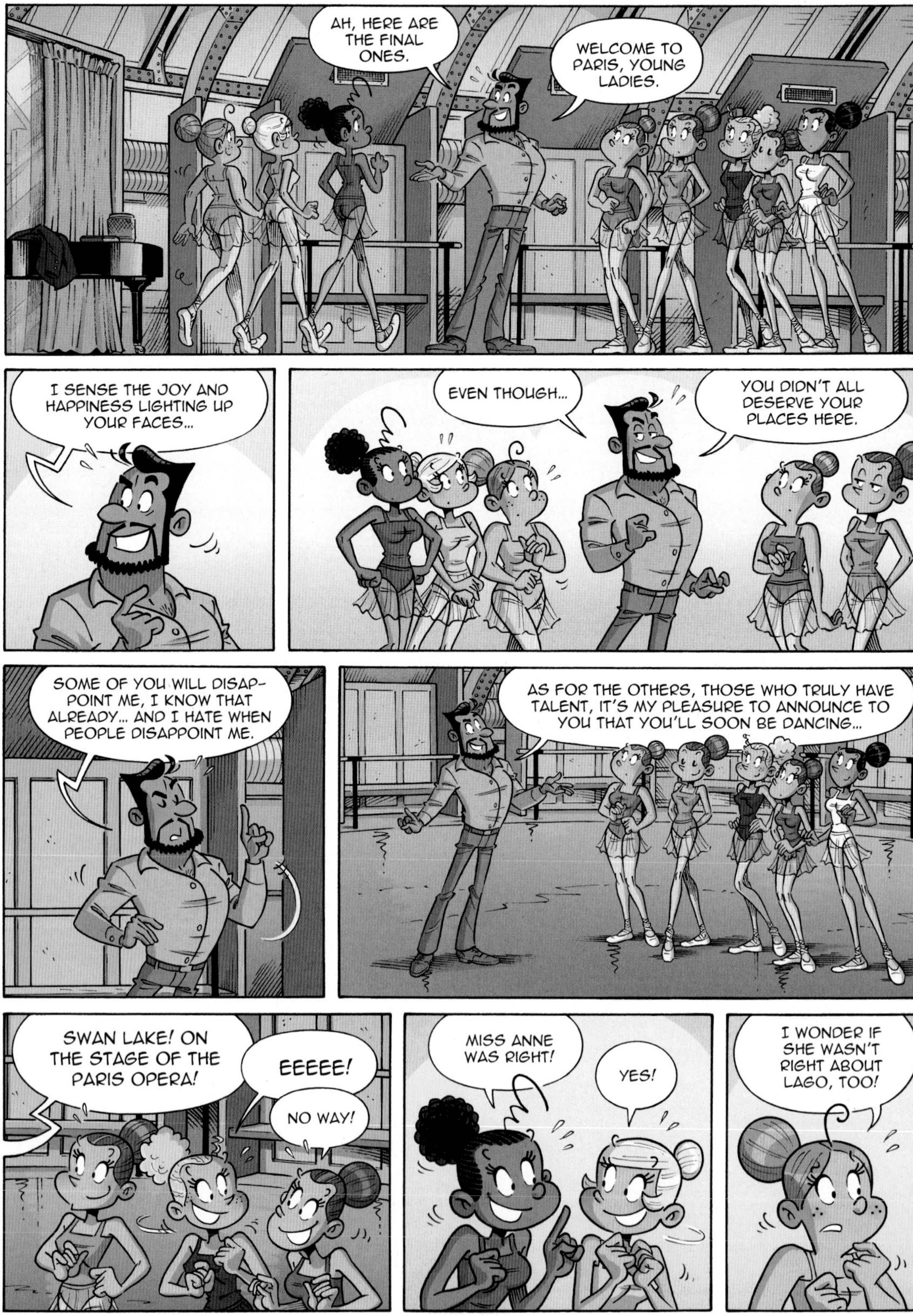

AH, HERE ARE THE FINAL ONES.
WELCOME TO PARIS, YOUNG LADIES.
I SENSE THE JOY AND HAPPINESS LIGHTING UP YOUR FACES...
EVEN THOUGH...
YOU DIDN'T ALL DESERVE YOUR PLACES HERE.
SOME OF YOU WILL DISAP-POINT ME, I KNOW THAT ALREADY... AND I HATE WHEN PEOPLE DISAPPOINT ME.
AS FOR THE OTHERS, THOSE WHO TRULY HAVE TALENT, IT'S MY PLEASURE TO ANNOUNCE TO YOU THAT YOU'LL SOON BE DANCING...
SWAN LAKE! ON THE STAGE OF THE PARIS OPERA!
EEEEE!
NO WAY!
MISS ANNE WAS RIGHT!
YES!
I WONDER IF SHE WASN'T RIGHT ABOUT LAGO, TOO!

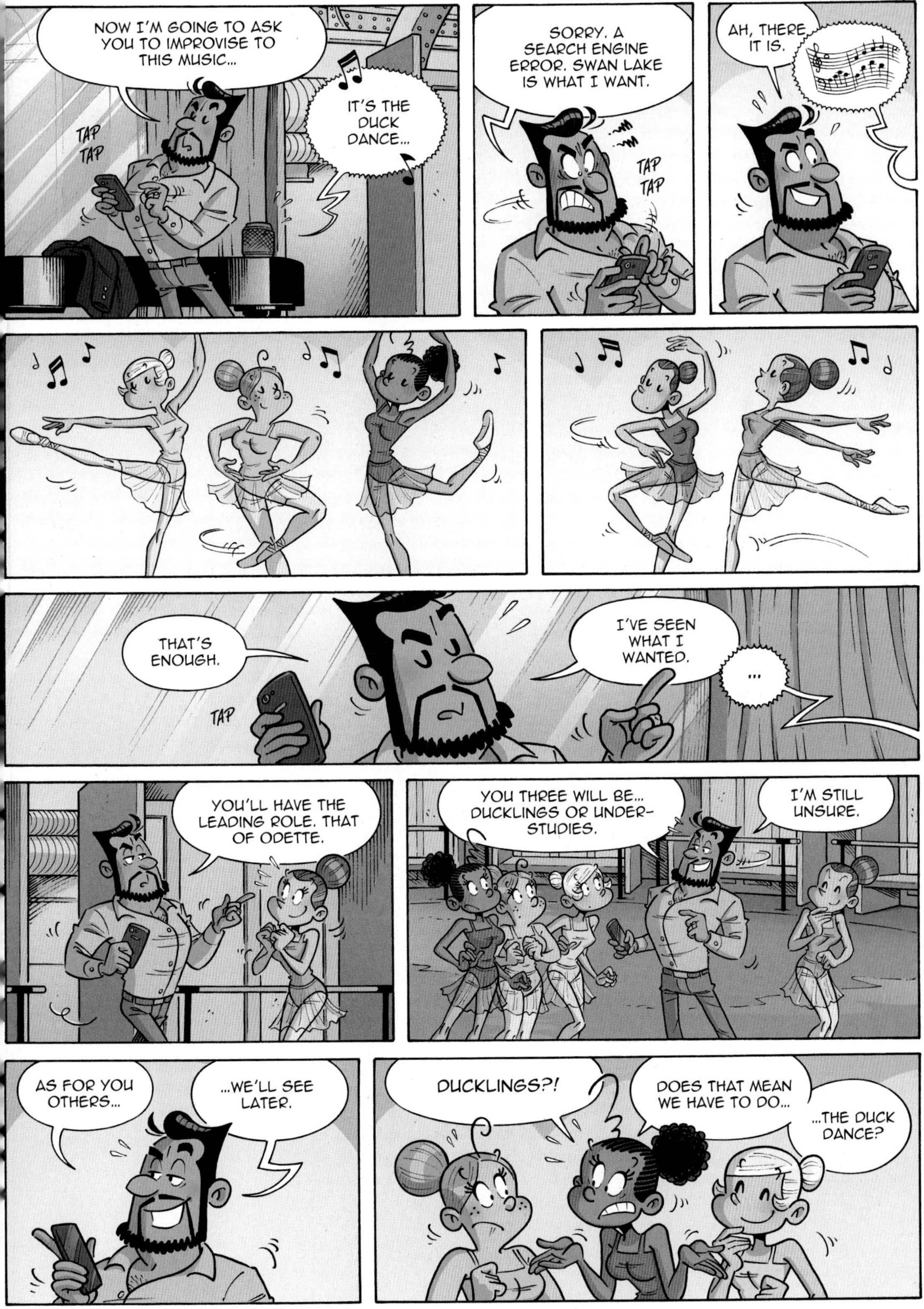
NOW I'M GOING TO ASK YOU TO IMPROVISE TO THIS MUSIC...
TAP TAP
IT'S THE DUCK DANCE...
SORRY. A SEARCH ENGINE ERROR. SWAN LAKE IS WHAT I WANT.
TAP TAP
AH, THERE IT IS.
THAT'S ENOUGH.
TAP
I'VE SEEN WHAT I WANTED.
...
YOU'LL HAVE THE LEADING ROLE. THAT OF ODETTE.
YOU THREE WILL BE... DUCKLINGS OR UNDER-STUDIES.
I'M STILL UNSURE.
AS FOR YOU OTHERS...
...WE'LL SEE LATER.
DUCKLINGS?!
DOES THAT MEAN WE HAVE TO DO...
...THE DUCK DANCE?

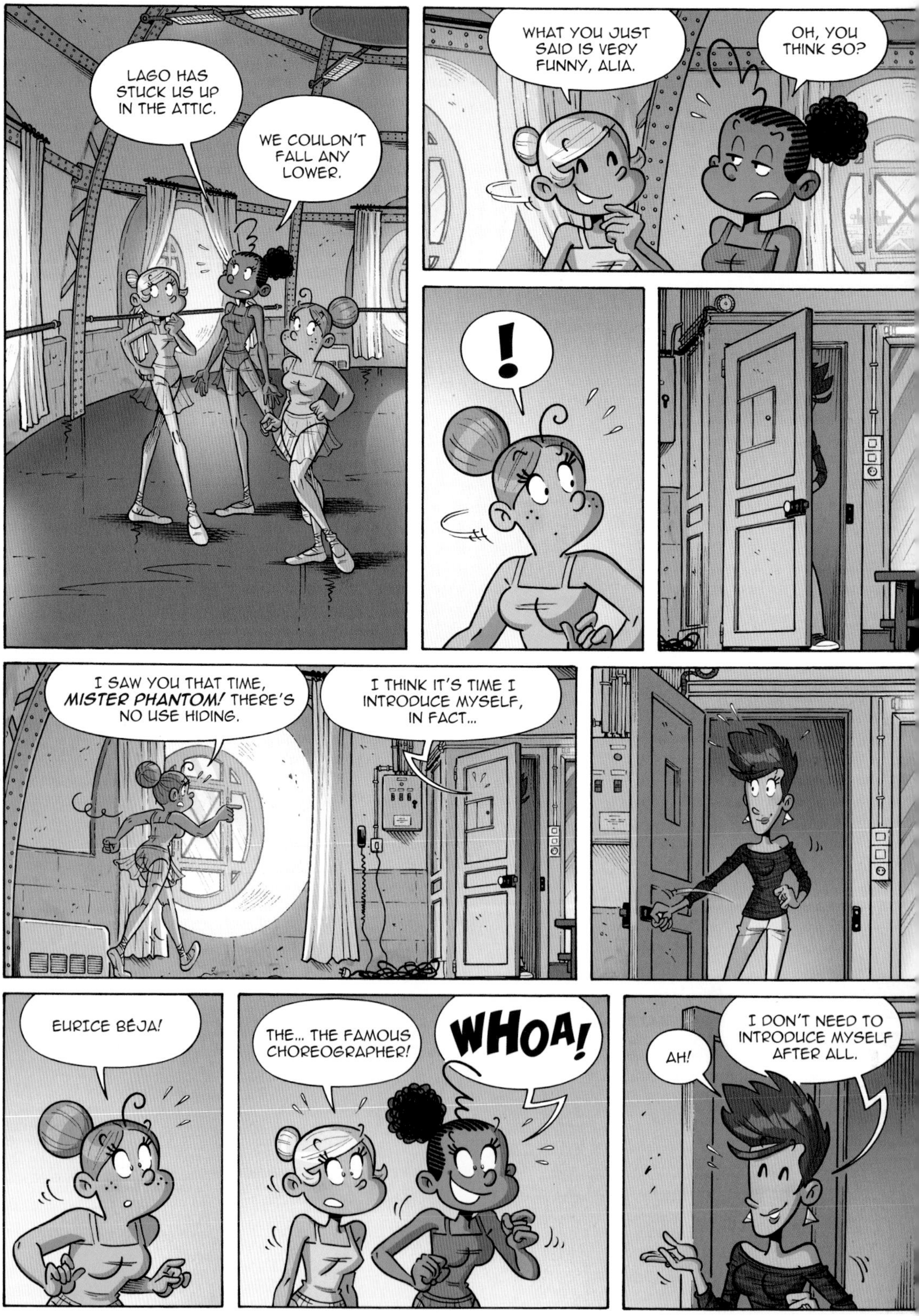
LAGO HAS STUCK US UP IN THE ATTIC.
WE COULDN'T FALL ANY LOWER.
WHAT YOU JUST SAID IS VERY FUNNY, ALIA.
OH, YOU THINK SO?
!
I SAW YOU THAT TIME, *MISTER PHANTOM!* THERE'S NO USE HIDING.
I THINK IT'S TIME I INTRODUCE MYSELF, IN FACT...
EURICE BÉJA!
THE... THE FAMOUS CHOREOGRAPHER!
WHOA!
AH!
I DON'T NEED TO INTRODUCE MYSELF AFTER ALL.

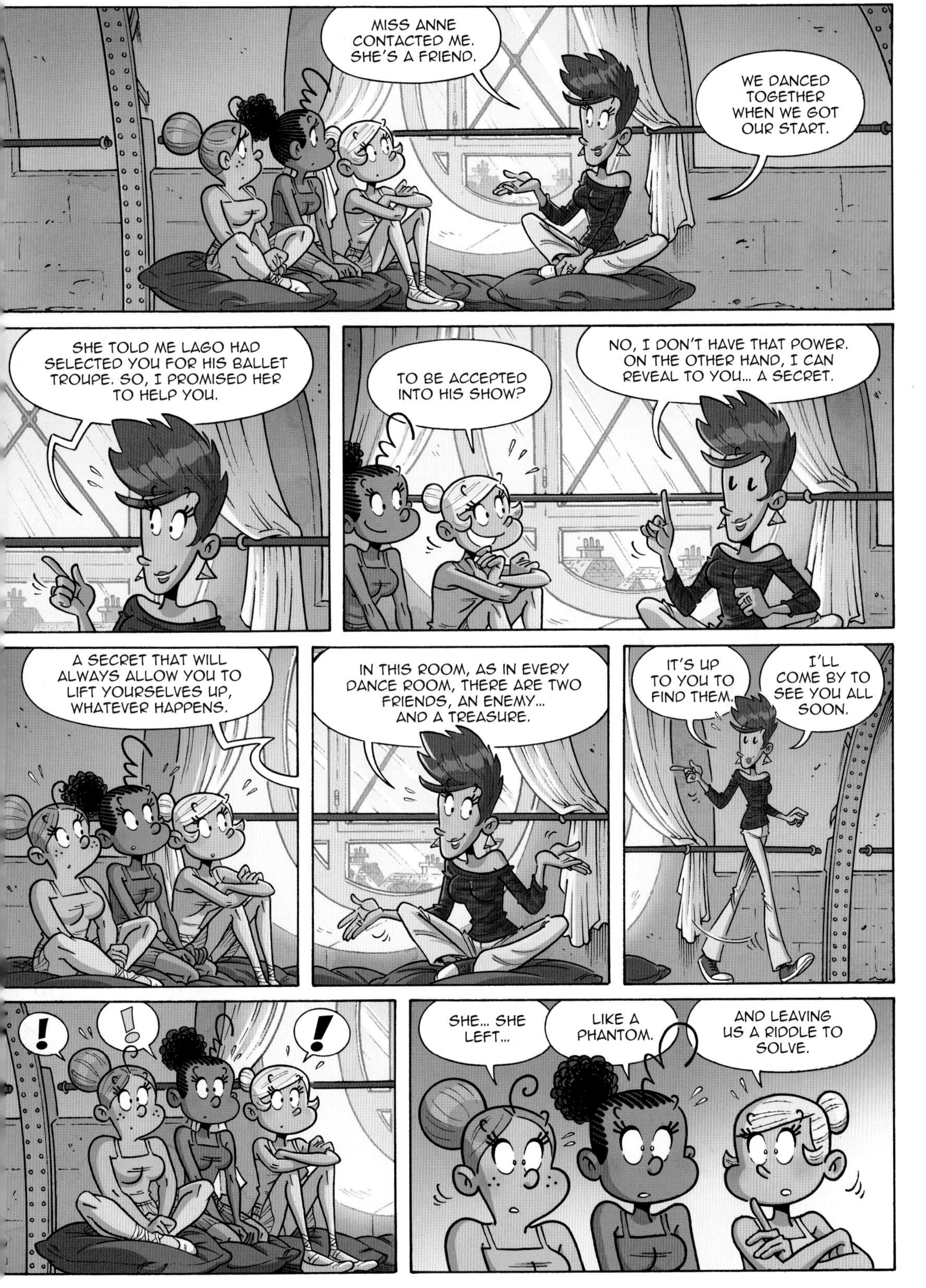
MISS ANNE CONTACTED ME. SHE'S A FRIEND.
WE DANCED TOGETHER WHEN WE GOT OUR START.
SHE TOLD ME LAGO HAD SELECTED YOU FOR HIS BALLET TROUPE. SO, I PROMISED HER TO HELP YOU.
TO BE ACCEPTED INTO HIS SHOW?
NO, I DON'T HAVE THAT POWER. ON THE OTHER HAND, I CAN REVEAL TO YOU... A SECRET.
A SECRET THAT WILL ALWAYS ALLOW YOU TO LIFT YOURSELVES UP, WHATEVER HAPPENS.
IN THIS ROOM, AS IN EVERY DANCE ROOM, THERE ARE TWO FRIENDS, AN ENEMY... AND A TREASURE.
IT'S UP TO YOU TO FIND THEM.
I'LL COME BY TO SEE YOU ALL SOON.
!
!
!
SHE... SHE LEFT...
LIKE A PHANTOM.
AND LEAVING US A RIDDLE TO SOLVE.

DID YOU FIND ANYTHING?

NOTHING AT ALL.

SAME HERE.

WE'LL CONTINUE LATER...

...IT'S TIME TO GO EAT.

I DON'T UNDERSTAND WHY EURICE SAID: "IN THIS ROOM... AS IN EVERY DANCE ROOM..."

WHO'S THE BEST?

THE ONE WHO GOT THE LEAD ROLE... HMMM?

!

WHY, YES!

I'VE FOUND THE ENEMY!

CARLA?!

DON'T TELL ME THERE'S ONE IN EVERY DANCE ROOM!

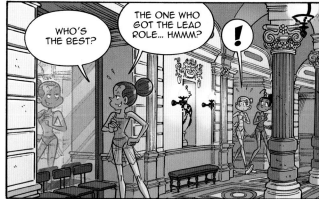

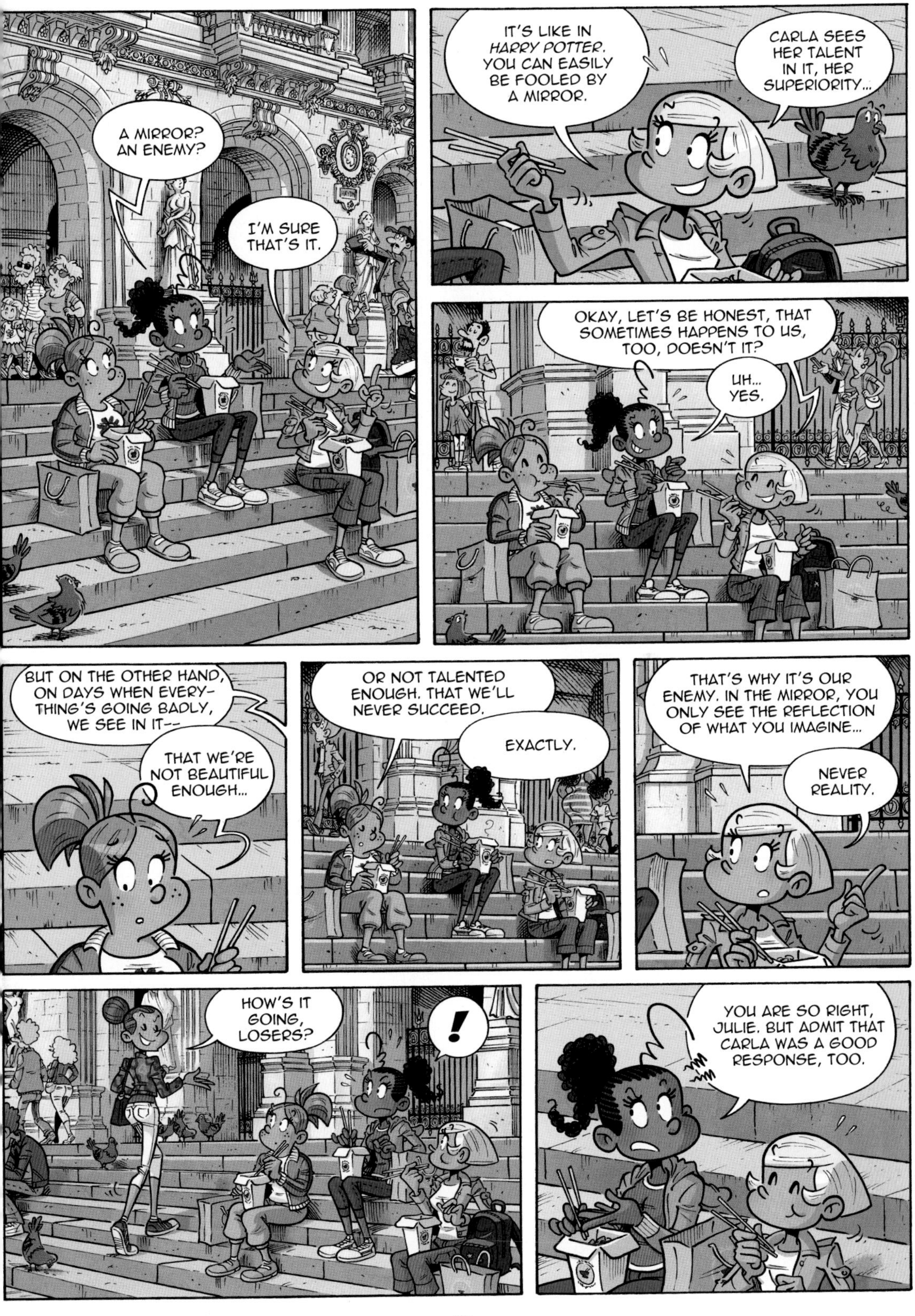
A MIRROR? AN ENEMY?
I'M SURE THAT'S IT.
IT'S LIKE IN *HARRY POTTER*. YOU CAN EASILY BE FOOLED BY A MIRROR.
CARLA SEES HER TALENT IN IT, HER SUPERIORITY...
OKAY, LET'S BE HONEST, THAT SOMETIMES HAPPENS TO US, TOO, DOESN'T IT?
UH... YES.
BUT ON THE OTHER HAND, ON DAYS WHEN EVERYTHING'S GOING BADLY, WE SEE IN IT--
THAT WE'RE NOT BEAUTIFUL ENOUGH...
OR NOT TALENTED ENOUGH. THAT WE'LL NEVER SUCCEED.
EXACTLY.
THAT'S WHY IT'S OUR ENEMY. IN THE MIRROR, YOU ONLY SEE THE REFLECTION OF WHAT YOU IMAGINE...
NEVER REALITY.
HOW'S IT GOING, LOSERS?
!
YOU ARE SO RIGHT, JULIE. BUT ADMIT THAT CARLA WAS A GOOD RESPONSE, TOO.

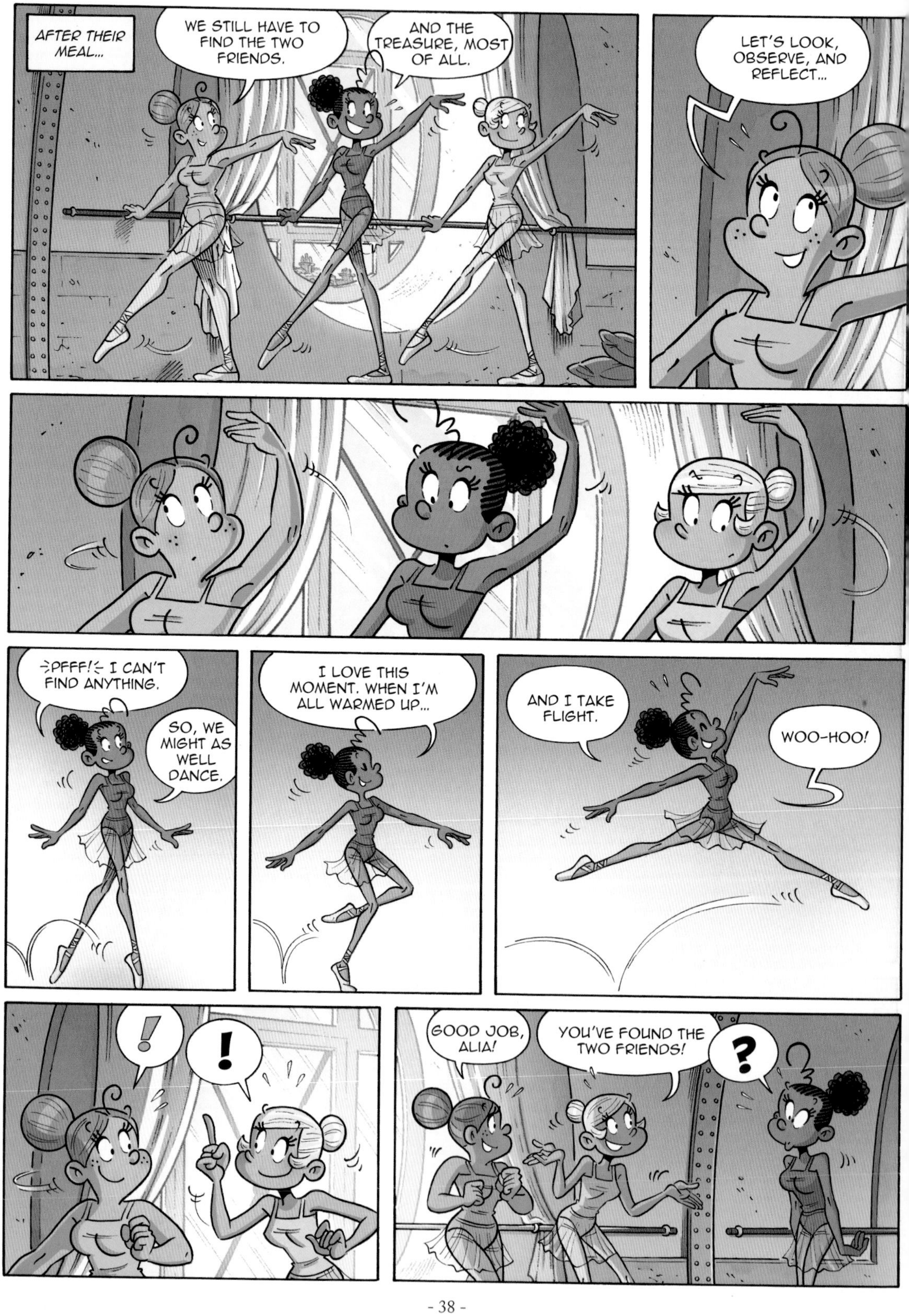
AFTER THEIR MEAL...
WE STILL HAVE TO FIND THE TWO FRIENDS.
AND THE TREASURE, MOST OF ALL.
LET'S LOOK, OBSERVE, AND REFLECT...
PFFF! I CAN'T FIND ANYTHING.
SO, WE MIGHT AS WELL DANCE.
I LOVE THIS MOMENT. WHEN I'M ALL WARMED UP...
AND I TAKE FLIGHT.
WOO-HOO!
!
!
GOOD JOB, ALIA!
YOU'VE FOUND THE TWO FRIENDS!
?

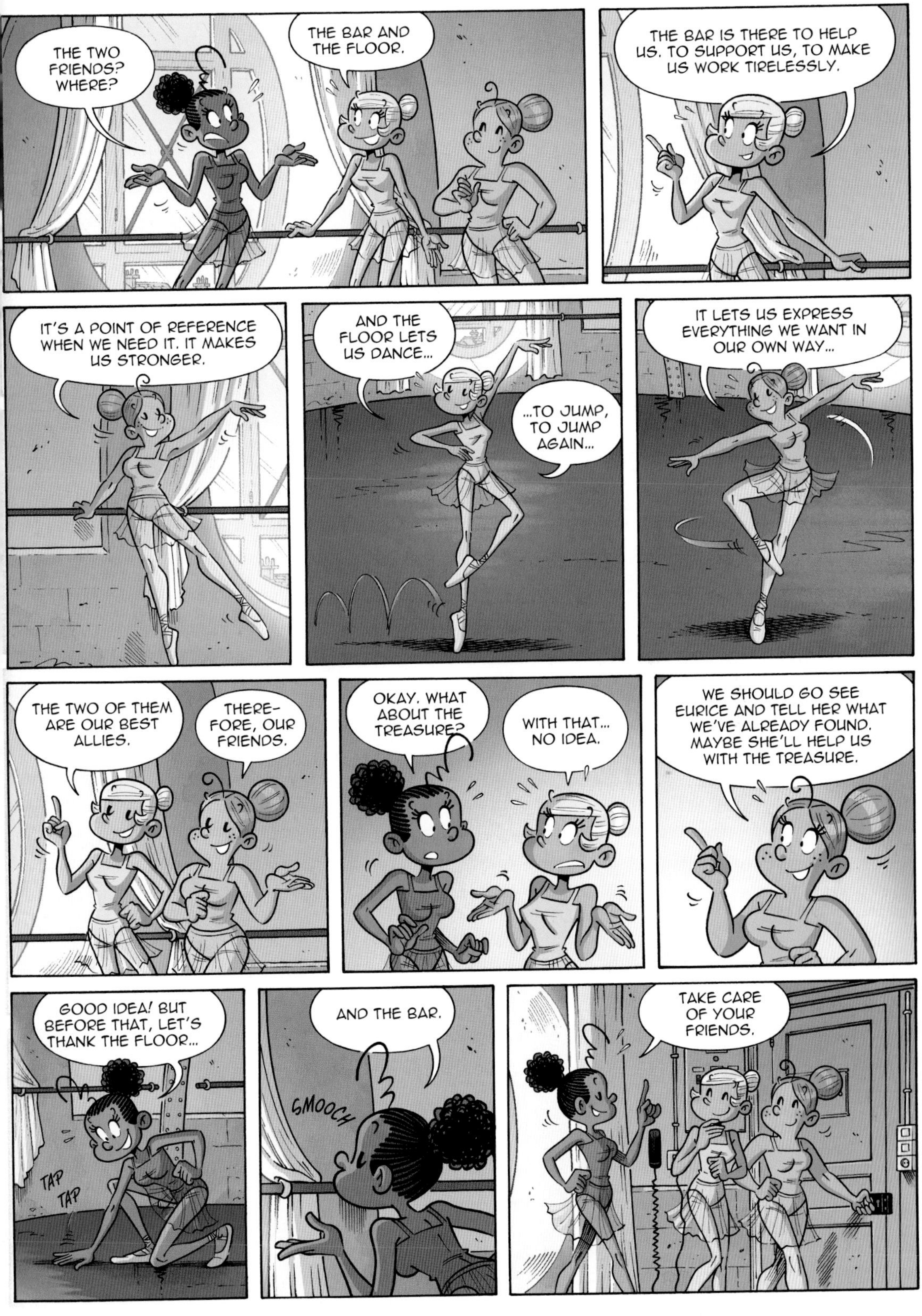
THE TWO FRIENDS? WHERE?
THE BAR AND THE FLOOR.
THE BAR IS THERE TO HELP US. TO SUPPORT US, TO MAKE US WORK TIRELESSLY.
IT'S A POINT OF REFERENCE WHEN WE NEED IT. IT MAKES US STRONGER.
AND THE FLOOR LETS US DANCE...
...TO JUMP, TO JUMP AGAIN...
IT LETS US EXPRESS EVERYTHING WE WANT IN OUR OWN WAY...
THE TWO OF THEM ARE OUR BEST ALLIES.
THERE-FORE, OUR FRIENDS.
OKAY. WHAT ABOUT THE TREASURE?
WITH THAT... NO IDEA.
WE SHOULD GO SEE EURICE AND TELL HER WHAT WE'VE ALREADY FOUND. MAYBE SHE'LL HELP US WITH THE TREASURE.
GOOD IDEA! BUT BEFORE THAT, LET'S THANK THE FLOOR...
TAP TAP
AND THE BAR.
SMOOCH
TAKE CARE OF YOUR FRIENDS.

ARE WE ALLOWED IN HERE?

I DON'T THINK SO.

WE MUST HAVE GOTTEN TURNED AROUND...

!

EURICE! SHE'S INVENTING A NEW CHOREOGRAPHY.

THAT'S JUST... SUBLIME.

CREEAK CREEAK CREEAK

!

SOMEONE'S COMING!

LET'S HIDE, QUICK!

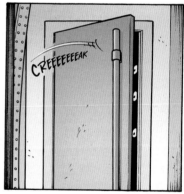

CREEEEEEEAK

!?

CROUIK! CROUIK!

OH, IT'S YOU, EURICE.

HELLO, LAGO.

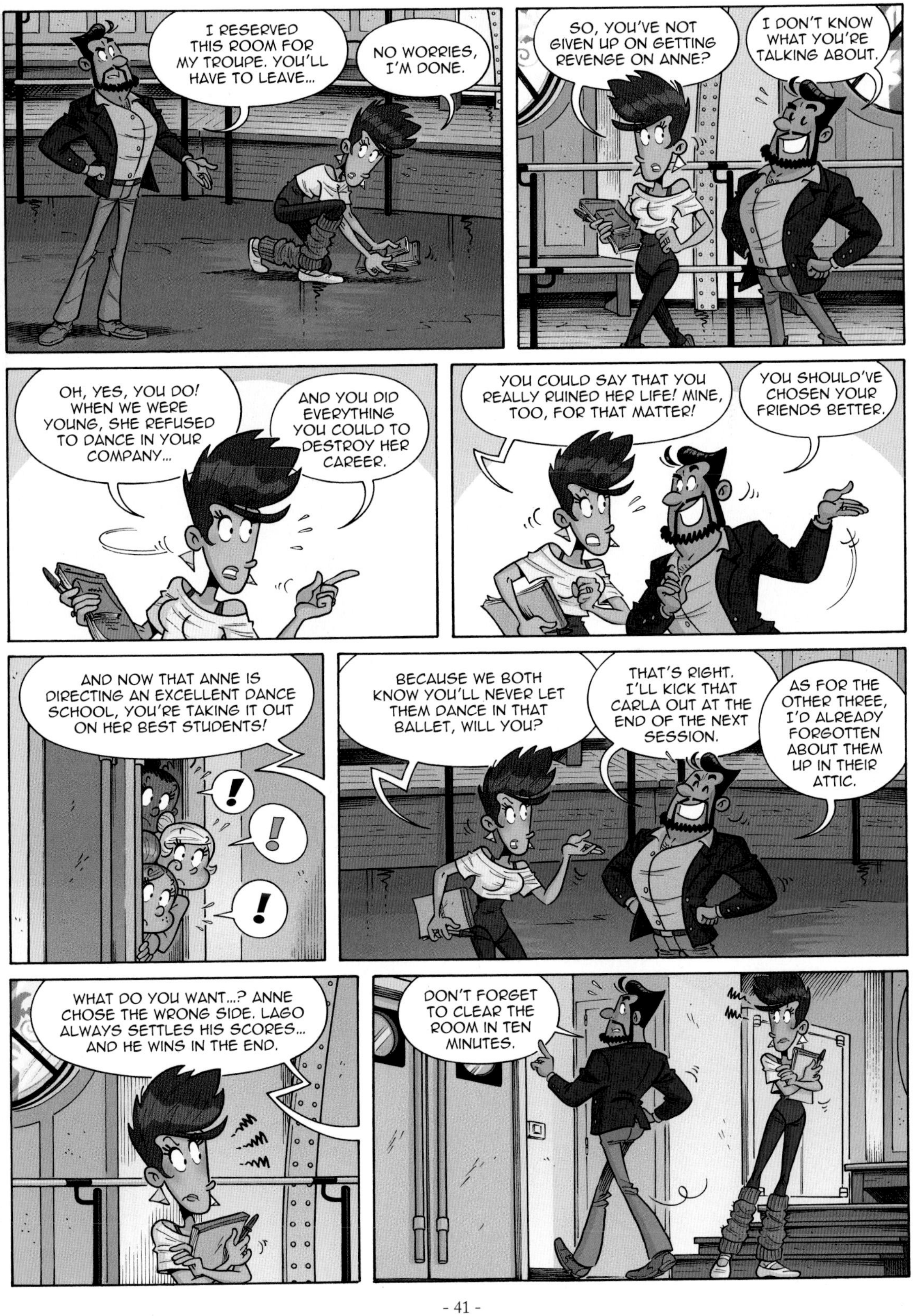
I RESERVED THIS ROOM FOR MY TROUPE. YOU'LL HAVE TO LEAVE...
NO WORRIES, I'M DONE.
SO, YOU'VE NOT GIVEN UP ON GETTING REVENGE ON ANNE?
I DON'T KNOW WHAT YOU'RE TALKING ABOUT.
OH, YES, YOU DO! WHEN WE WERE YOUNG, SHE REFUSED TO DANCE IN YOUR COMPANY...
AND YOU DID EVERYTHING YOU COULD TO DESTROY HER CAREER.
YOU COULD SAY THAT YOU REALLY RUINED HER LIFE! MINE, TOO, FOR THAT MATTER!
YOU SHOULD'VE CHOSEN YOUR FRIENDS BETTER.
AND NOW THAT ANNE IS DIRECTING AN EXCELLENT DANCE SCHOOL, YOU'RE TAKING IT OUT ON HER BEST STUDENTS!
!
!
!
BECAUSE WE BOTH KNOW YOU'LL NEVER LET THEM DANCE IN THAT BALLET, WILL YOU?
THAT'S RIGHT. I'LL KICK THAT CARLA OUT AT THE END OF THE NEXT SESSION.
AS FOR THE OTHER THREE, I'D ALREADY FORGOTTEN ABOUT THEM UP IN THEIR ATTIC.
WHAT DO YOU WANT...? ANNE CHOSE THE WRONG SIDE. LAGO ALWAYS SETTLES HIS SCORES... AND HE WINS IN THE END.
DON'T FORGET TO CLEAR THE ROOM IN TEN MINUTES.

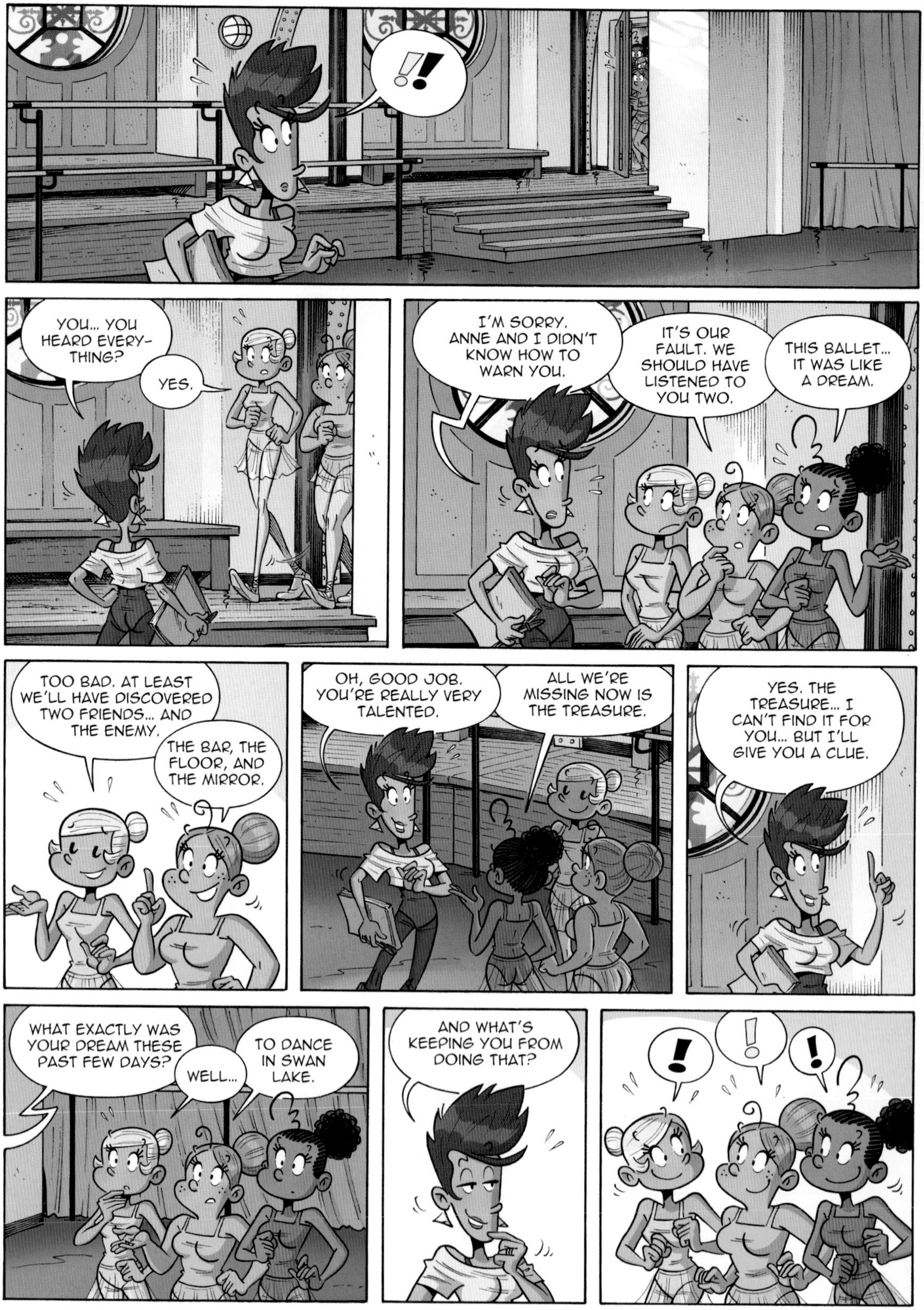
!!
YOU... YOU HEARD EVERYTHING?
YES.
I'M SORRY. ANNE AND I DIDN'T KNOW HOW TO WARN YOU.
IT'S OUR FAULT. WE SHOULD HAVE LISTENED TO YOU TWO.
THIS BALLET... IT WAS LIKE A DREAM.
TOO BAD. AT LEAST WE'LL HAVE DISCOVERED TWO FRIENDS... AND THE ENEMY.
THE BAR, THE FLOOR, AND THE MIRROR.
OH, GOOD JOB. YOU'RE REALLY VERY TALENTED.
ALL WE'RE MISSING NOW IS THE TREASURE.
YES. THE TREASURE... I CAN'T FIND IT FOR YOU... BUT I'LL GIVE YOU A CLUE.
WHAT EXACTLY WAS YOUR DREAM THESE PAST FEW DAYS?
WELL...
TO DANCE IN SWAN LAKE.
AND WHAT'S KEEPING YOU FROM DOING THAT?
!
!
!

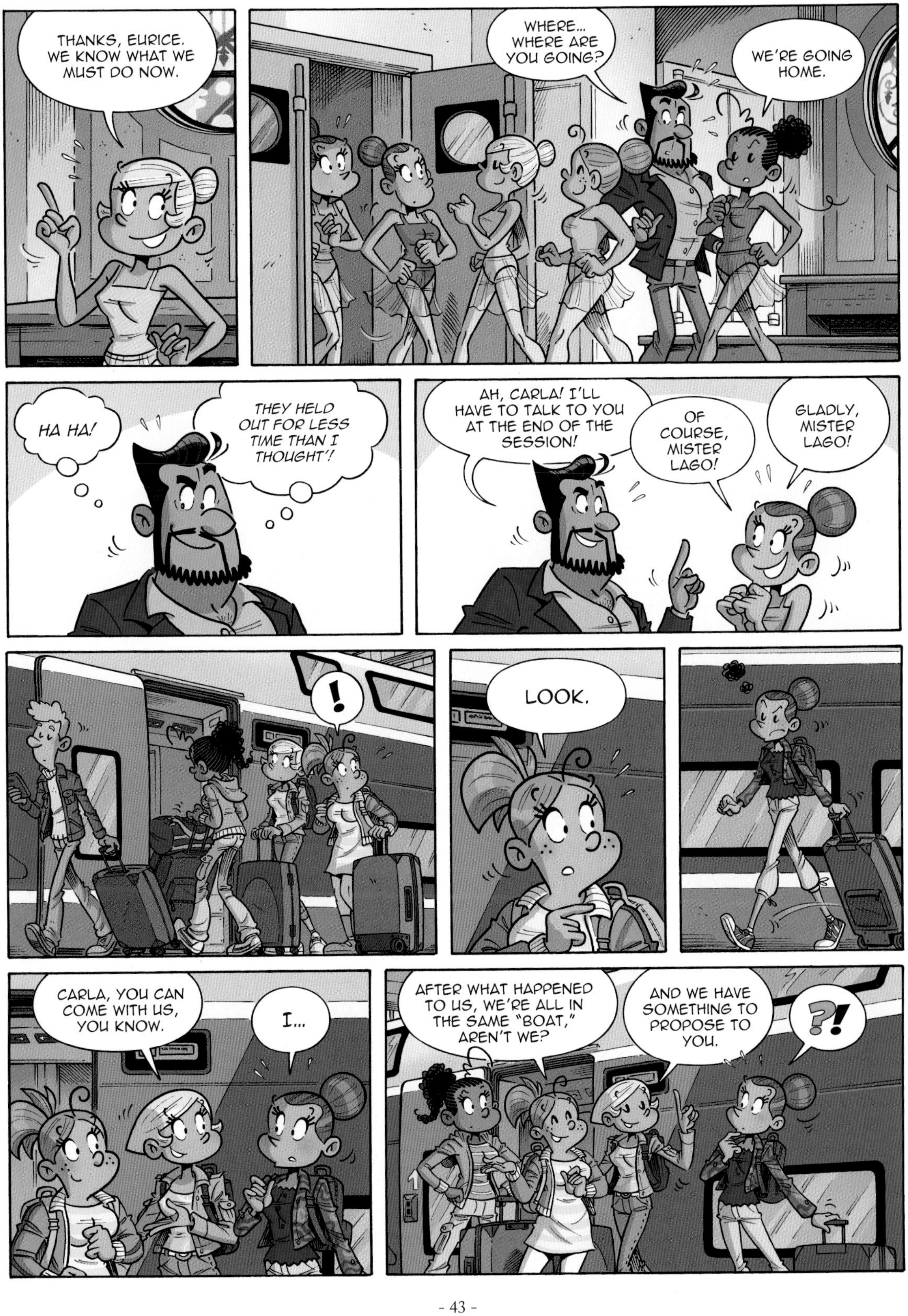
THANKS, EURICE. WE KNOW WHAT WE MUST DO NOW.
WHERE... WHERE ARE YOU GOING?
WE'RE GOING HOME.
HA HA!
THEY HELD OUT FOR LESS TIME THAN I THOUGHT'!
AH, CARLA! I'LL HAVE TO TALK TO YOU AT THE END OF THE SESSION!
OF COURSE, MISTER LAGO!
GLADLY, MISTER LAGO!
!
LOOK.
CARLA, YOU CAN COME WITH US, YOU KNOW.
I...
AFTER WHAT HAPPENED TO US, WE'RE ALL IN THE SAME "BOAT," AREN'T WE?
AND WE HAVE SOMETHING TO PROPOSE TO YOU.
?!

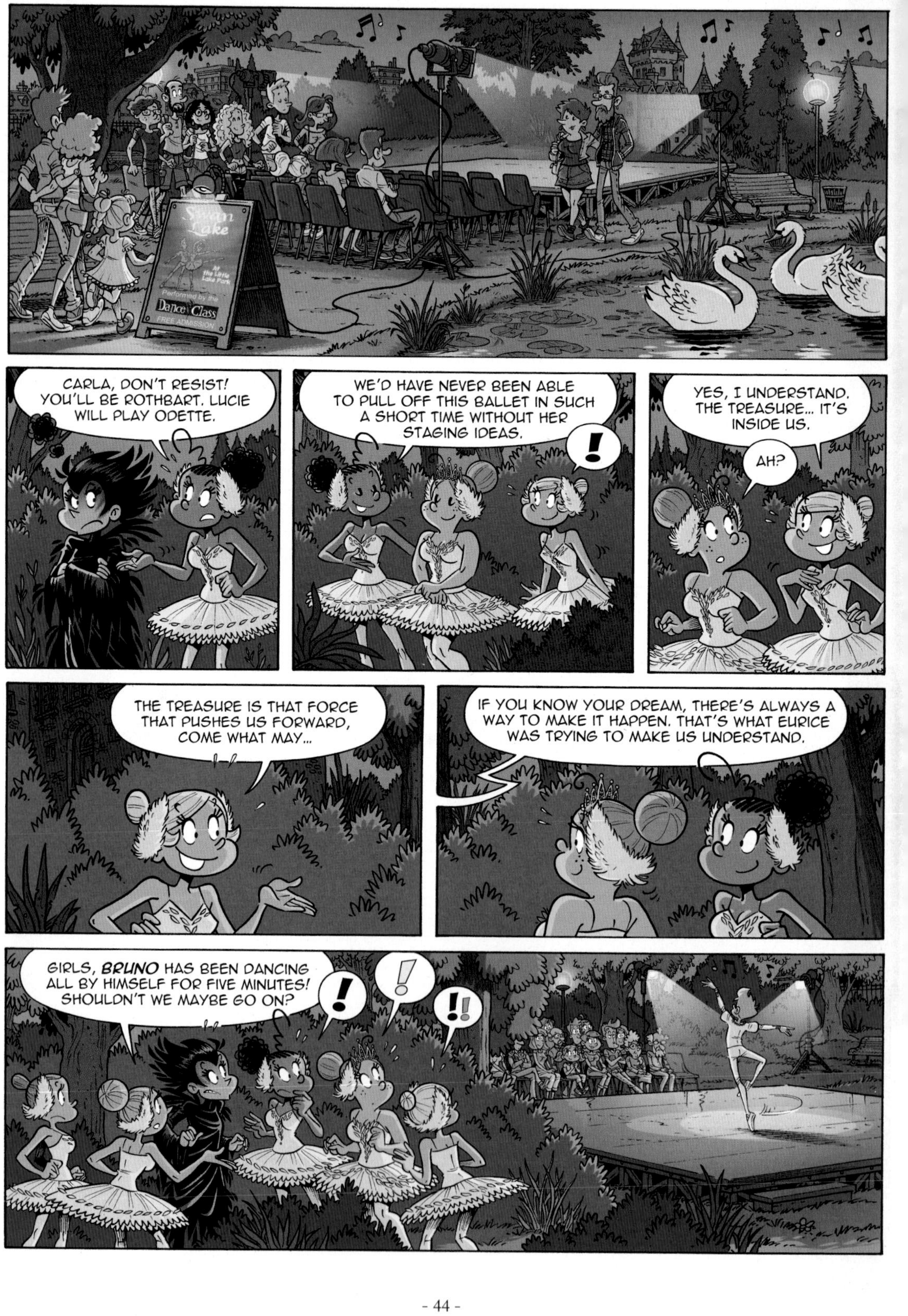

Swan Lake
At the Little Lake Park
Performed by the
Dance Class
FREE ADMISSION
CARLA, DON'T RESIST! YOU'LL BE ROTHBART. LUCIE WILL PLAY ODETTE.
WE'D HAVE NEVER BEEN ABLE TO PULL OFF THIS BALLET IN SUCH A SHORT TIME WITHOUT HER STAGING IDEAS.
!
YES, I UNDERSTAND. THE TREASURE... IT'S INSIDE US.
AH?
THE TREASURE IS THAT FORCE THAT PUSHES US FORWARD, COME WHAT MAY...
IF YOU KNOW YOUR DREAM, THERE'S ALWAYS A WAY TO MAKE IT HAPPEN. THAT'S WHAT EURICE WAS TRYING TO MAKE US UNDERSTAND.
GIRLS, **BRUNO** HAS BEEN DANCING ALL BY HIMSELF FOR FIVE MINUTES! SHOULDN'T WE MAYBE GO ON?
!
!
!!

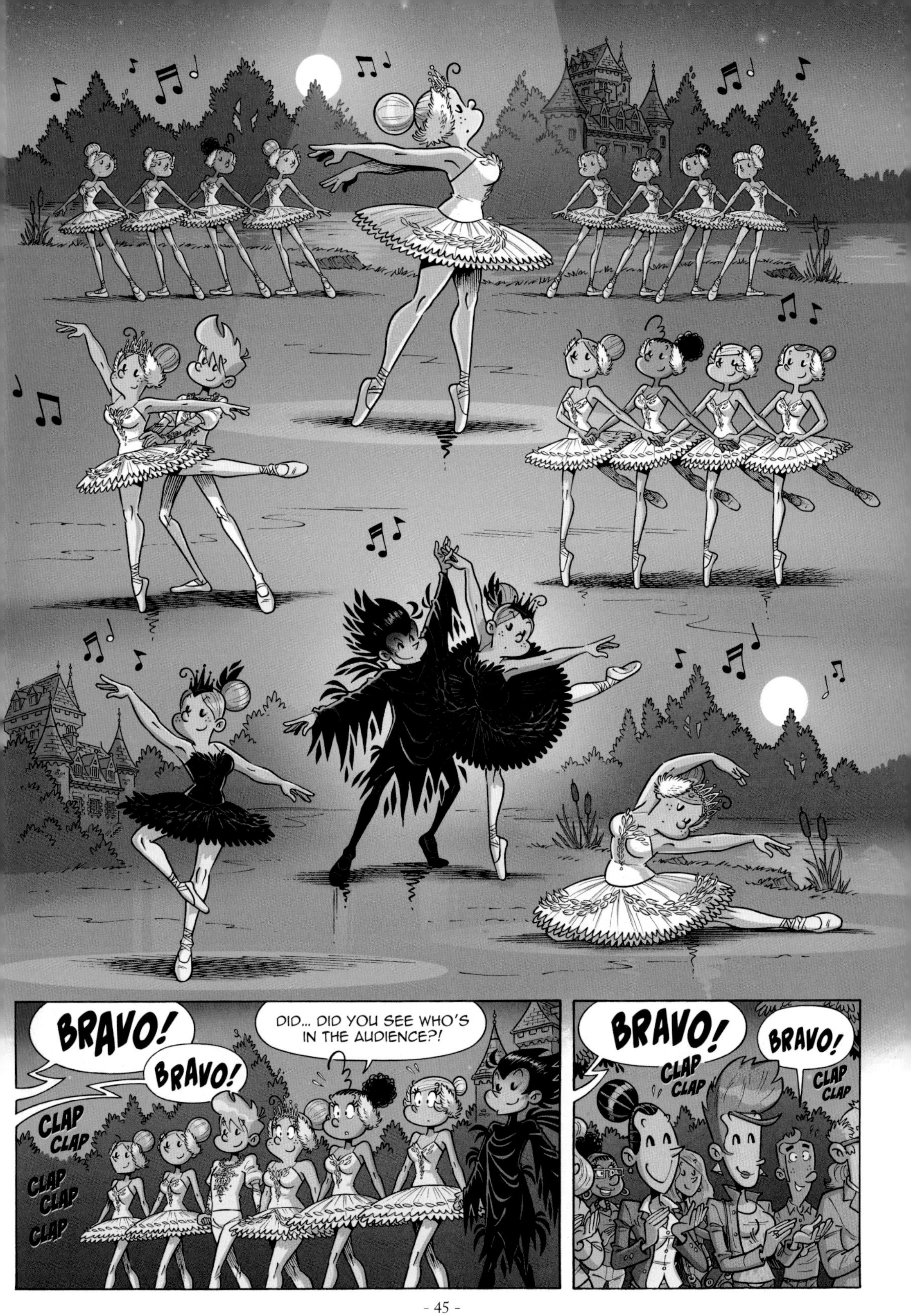
BRAVO!
BRAVO!
CLAP CLAP
CLAP CLAP CLAP
DID... DID YOU SEE WHO'S IN THE AUDIENCE?!
BRAVO!
CLAP CLAP
BRAVO!
CLAP CLAP

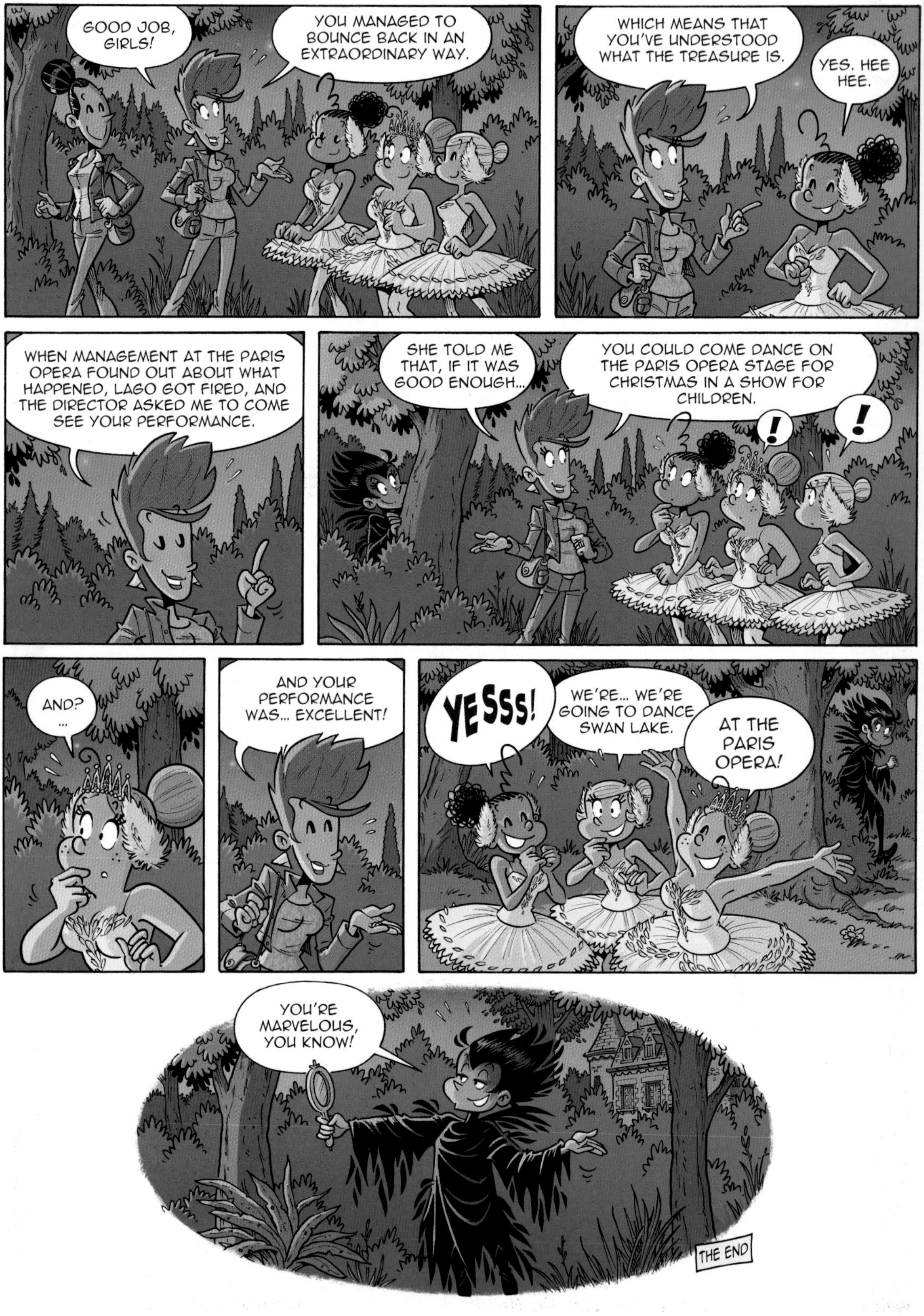
GOOD JOB, GIRLS!
YOU MANAGED TO BOUNCE BACK IN AN EXTRAORDINARY WAY.
WHICH MEANS THAT YOU'VE UNDERSTOOD WHAT THE TREASURE IS.
YES. HEE HEE.
WHEN MANAGEMENT AT THE PARIS OPERA FOUND OUT ABOUT WHAT HAPPENED, LAGO GOT FIRED, AND THE DIRECTOR ASKED ME TO COME SEE YOUR PERFORMANCE.
SHE TOLD ME THAT, IF IT WAS GOOD ENOUGH...
YOU COULD COME DANCE ON THE PARIS OPERA STAGE FOR CHRISTMAS IN A SHOW FOR CHILDREN.
!
!
AND? ...
AND YOUR PERFORMANCE WAS... EXCELLENT!
YESSS!
WE'RE... WE'RE GOING TO DANCE SWAN LAKE.
AT THE PARIS OPERA!
YOU'RE MARVELOUS, YOU KNOW!
THE END

WATCH OUT FOR PAPERCUTZ

"Hello, I Must Be Going." –sung by Groucho Marx as Captain Spaulding in the 1930 film, Animal Crackers

Welcome to the toe-pointing, thirteenth DANCE CLASS graphic novel, "Swan Lake," by Béka and Crip, brought to you by Papercutz—those folks dedicated to publishing great graphic novels for all ages where you can discover imaginative new worlds. I'm Jim Salicrup, the erstwhile Papercutz Editor-in-Chief and Current Consultant, here to share some really big Papercutz news…

Alas, it was already reported on Forbes.com that Papercutz has been purchased by Mad Cave Studios. This is great, as it means Papercutz will not only continue to bring you the graphic novels you already love, but will also launch even more. And Mad Cave Studios has the resources to do an even better job of promoting and marketing Papercutz and getting our graphic novels onto the shelves of even more booksellers and libraries, both print and digital editions.

The new Papercutz Editorial Director is Rex Ogle, who has worked at Marvel and DC Comics, as well as Scholastic and Little Brown for Young Readers. He's worked on everything from *LEGO* and *Minecraft* to *Star Wars* and *Buffy the Vampire Slayer*. When he's not editing books, he's either reading or writing them. Joining Rex will be Senior Editor Zohra Ashpari, who was previously an editor at Tapas Media and has worked within the editorial departments of Scholastic and Tor Books. And completing the new editorial team will be Editor Stephanie Brooks, who started as an editorial intern at NBM before becoming my Assistant Managing Editor at Papercutz. Welcome, Rex, Zohra, and Stephanie! The future of Papercutz is certainly in good hands!

Over twenty years ago, graphic novel pioneer and NBM publisher, Terry Nantier, had the brilliant concept of starting yet another graphic novel publishing company. When he originally launched NBM, the idea of comics for adults was revolutionary in the United States. After successfully proving that concept could succeed, he noticed that almost every comics publisher was then aiming their comics to the adult audience, virtually abandoning kids. That's when Terry realized that there should be comics for kids again, especially for girls, and the idea for Papercutz was born. The name Papercutz was dreamed up by Terry's daughter Sylvia, who specifically requested that it not be spelled with a Z at the end, but you know how dads can be. That's also around the time that Terry asked me to be his publishing partner and Editor-in-Chief in this crazy new venture, for which I readily agreed. I had started at Marvel Comics in 1972 when I was fifteen years old (2022 marked my 50th anniversary of working in comics!). The year before that I was one of the kids at *Kids Magazine*. Seems I've always been interested in comics for kids. Even at Marvel I had written and then edited SPIDEY SUPER STORIES, a kids version of *Spider-Man* comics designed to help children read, co-produced with the producers of *Sesame Street* and *The Electric*

Company, the Children's Television Workshop. And there are countless other kids-oriented projects that I worked on over the years.

The first Papercutz comicbook, THE HARDY BOYS, was published in 2004, and in 2005, the first Papercutz graphic novels, THE HARDY BOYS and NANCY DREW saw print. And we've been at it ever since, through a world-wide Great Recession in 2008 and the recent global Covid Pandemic. But after almost twenty years Terry and I decided it was time for others to take Papercutz up to the next level, and that's where Mad Cave Studios comes in. While there was virtually no competition in the kids' graphic novel category when we started, now almost every comics and book publisher is producing graphic novels for kids. Mad Cave Studios is better equipped to handle that kind of fierce competition.

For Terry and me, it's a little like Papercutz is one of our children that has grown up and is going off to college. While we both will be sticking around for a while as consultants to make the transition go as smoothly as possible, eventually we'll be moving on, leaving our baby in the very capable hands of Mad Cave Studios. While I may be leaving Papercutz, I'm certainly not leaving comics. There've been may other projects I've been hoping to work on, but Papercutz had been taking up almost every waking hour of my time. Now I'll be free to work on those projects.

There are way too many people I'd like to thank for making my time at Papercutz over the years so wonderful. Terry, of course, the best publishing partner I could ever imagine! All of our writers, artists, letterers, colorists, production people, and of course, my invaluable, hard-working Managing Editors Michael Petranek, Bethany Bryan, Suzannah Rowntree, Jeff Whitman, and Stephanie Brooks. And of course, all of you, the Papercutz fans who have supported us over the years, with a special shout out to Rachel Boden, one our biggest fans.

This will be my final *Watch Out for Papercutz* column in DANCE CLASS, but in light of the great news regarding Mad Cave Studios taking over, may my last words simply be, *watch out for Papercutz*—the best is yet to come!

Thanks,

Jim

STAY IN TOUCH!

WEB: papercutz.com
INSTAGRAM: @papercutzgn
TWITTER: @papercutzgn
YOUTUBE: @papercutzgn
FACEBOOK: PAPERCUTZGRAPHICNOVELS

Go to papercutz.com and sign up for the free Papercutz e-newsletter!

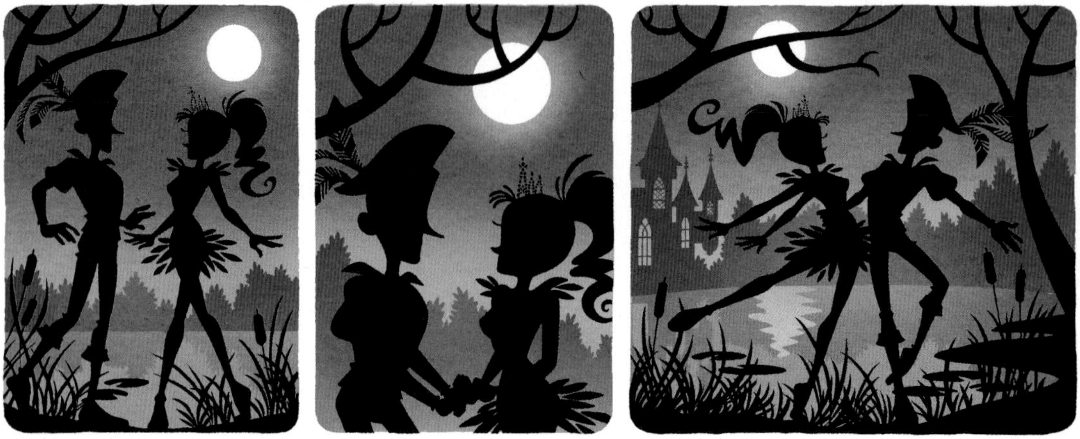

Dance Class Graphic Novels available from PAPERCUTZ

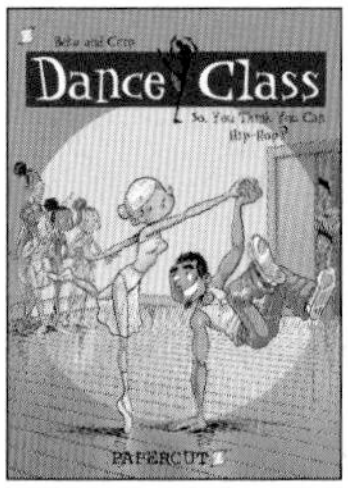
#1 "So, You Think You Can Hip-Hop?"

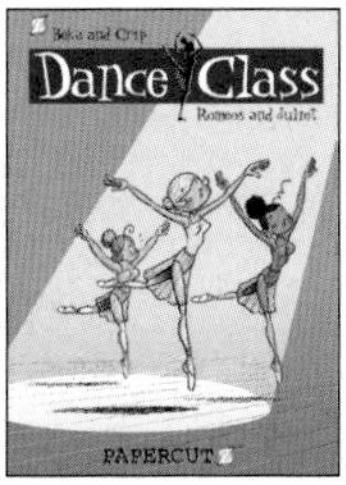
#2 "Romeos and Juliet"

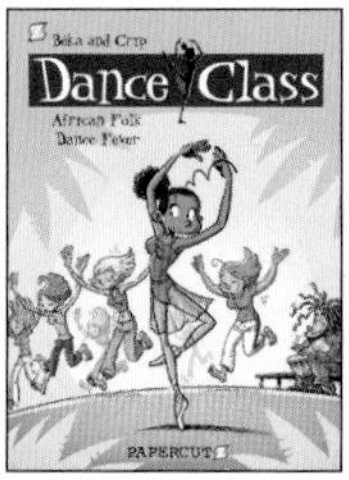
#3 "African Folk Dance Fever"

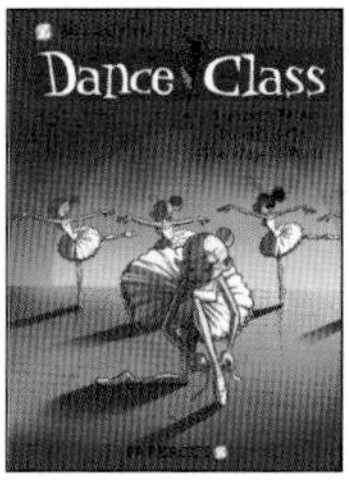
#4 "A Funny Thing Happened on the Way to Paris..."

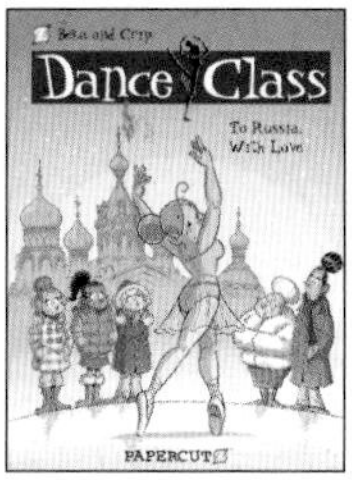
#5 "To Russia, With Love"

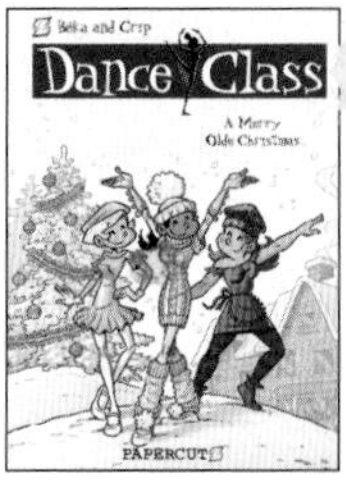
#6 "A Merry Olde Christmas"

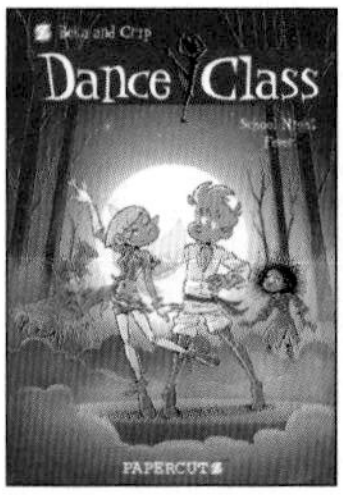
#7 "School Night Fever"

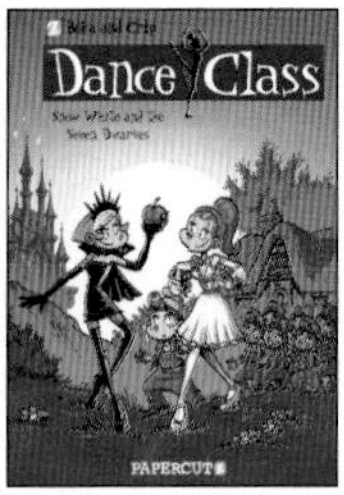
#8 "Snow White and the Seven Dwarves"

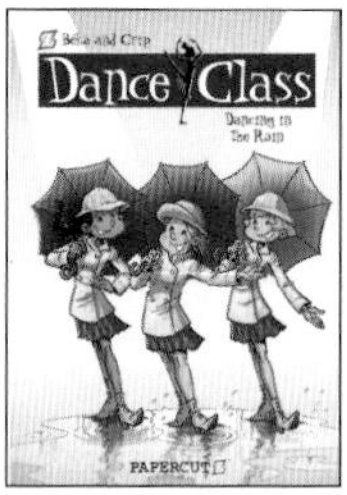
#9 "Dancing in the Rain"

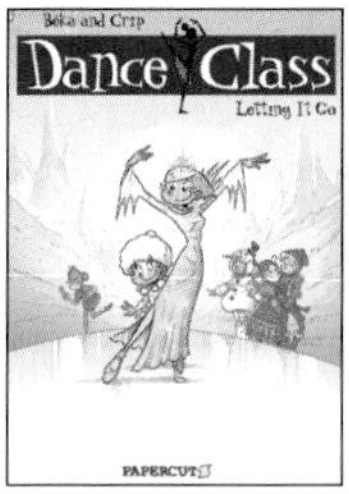
#10 "Letting It Go"

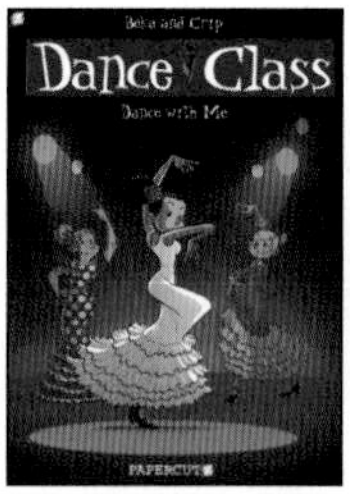
#11 "Dance with Me"

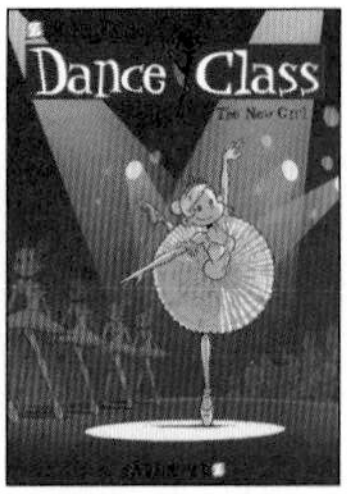
#12 "The New Girl"

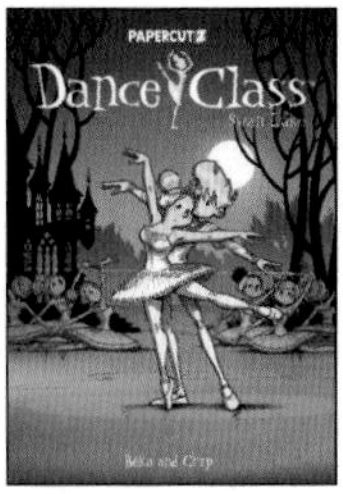
#13 "Swan Lake"

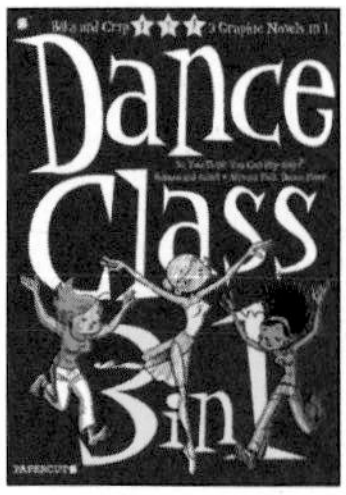
DANCE CLASS 3 IN 1 #1

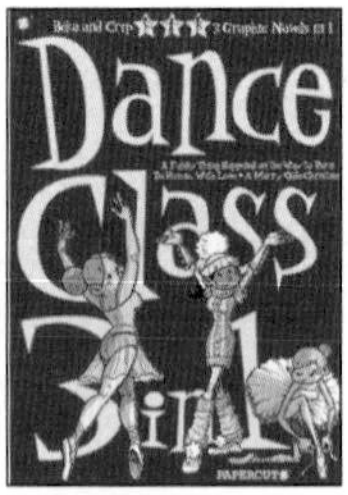
DANCE CLASS 3 IN 1 #2

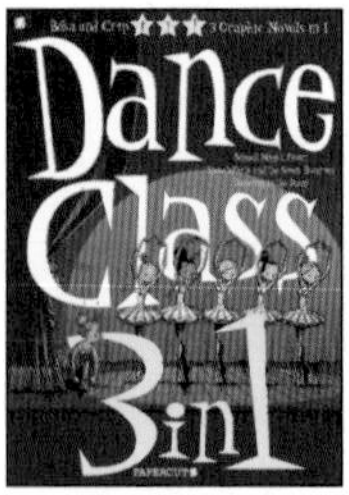
DANCE CLASS 3 IN 1 #3

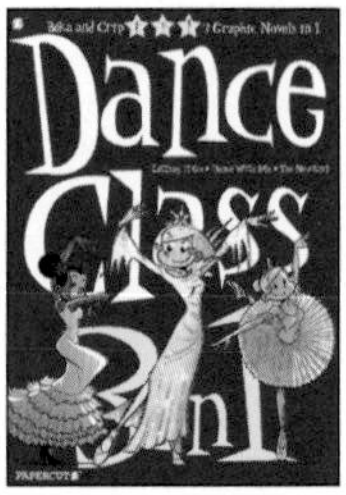
DANCE CLASS 3 IN 1 #4

SEE MORE AT PAPERCUTZ.COM • Also available digitally wherever e-books are sold.

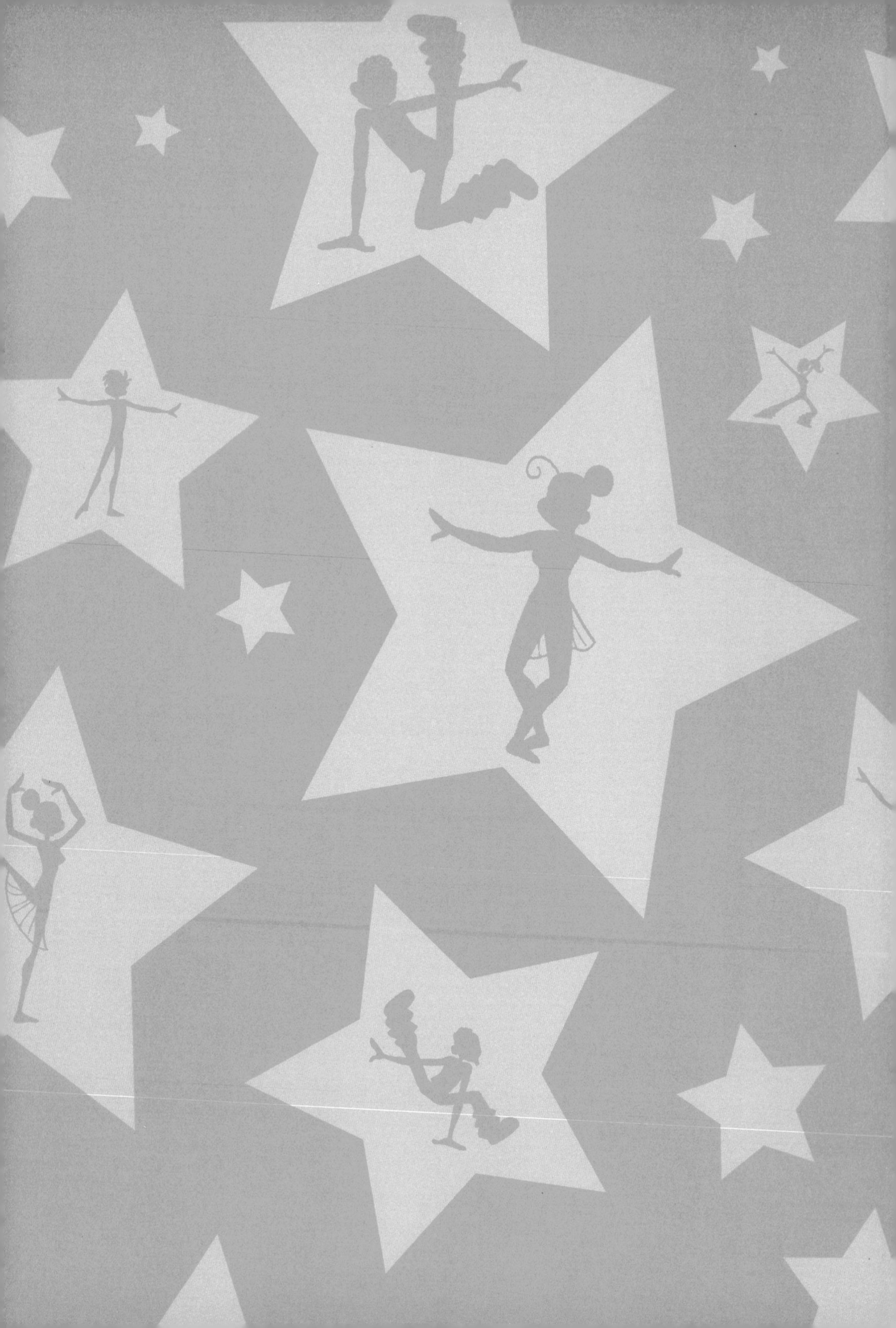